I0544722

DEAD STRIPPER STORAGE

BRYAN SMITH

Dead Stripper Storage copyright © 2018 by Bryan Smith. All rights reserved.

Grindhouse Press
PO BOX 521
Dayton, Ohio 45401

Grindhouse Press logo and all related artwork copyright © 2018 by Brandon Duncan. All rights reserved.

Cover design copyright Matthew Revert © 2018. All rights reserved.

Grindhouse Press #041
ISBN-10: 1-941918-33-6
ISBN-13: 978-1-941918-33-3

This is a work of fiction. All characters and events portrayed in this book are fictitious and any resemblance to real people or events is purely coincidental.

No part of this book may be reproduced, stored in a retrieval system, or transmitted in any form or by any means, including mechanical, electric, photocopying, recording, or otherwise, without the prior written permission of the publisher or author.

DEDICATION

In memory of that one deliriously drunken evening in 1994 in when I blundered my way into the strippers' dressing room at a Déjà vu in West Palm Beach. Good times. Until I puked all over that hotel room the next day. But that's another story.

Other titles by Bryan Smith

House of Blood
Rock and Roll Reform School Zombies
Darkened
Highways to Hell
The Dark Ones
Some Crazy Fucking Shit That Happened One Day
The Freakshow
Soultaker
Queen of Blood
Grimm Awakening
Blood and Whiskey
The Halloween Bride
The Diabolical Conspiracy
Deathbringer
Strange Ways
Slowly We Rot
Surrounded By Bastards
The Reborn
Bloodrush
All Hallow's Dead
Christmas Eve on Haunted Hill
Seven Deadly Tales of Terror
The Late Night Horror Show
Go Kill Crazy!
Wicked Kayla
Murder Squad
Last Day
Depraved
Depraved 2
Depraved 3
68 Kill
68 Kill Part 2
Kayla and The Devil (Kayla Monroe: Haunted World Book 1)
Kayla Undead (Kayla Monroe: Haunted World Book 2)
The Killing Kind
The Killing Kind 2

ONE

Pete Adler woke up feeling pretty good about life in general that Saturday morning. The sun was shining through his window blinds. Birds were chirping somewhere outside. It was a beautiful day. More importantly, the weekend was finally here. Workplace issues that had caused him to entertain fantasies of suicide by midweek had all been resolved in unexpectedly tidy fashion by the end of the day on Friday, lifting a psychological burden he'd been certain would continue to make his life an exercise in dreary misery for untold weeks and months to come.

Deliverance from this dark state of mind came in the form of the unexpected firing of Shane Watson, who had been escorted from the premises about a half hour prior to the normal end of the workday. This came in the wake of a long, closed-door meeting between Shane and his supervisor. Shane went into the meeting all smiles as usual, cracking jokes with his buddies as he moved between the rows of cubicles. His buddies laughed in their usual sheep-like way. Along the way, he mimed firing a gun at Pete, blowing at the tip of his upraised forefinger as if blowing smoke from the barrel of a pistol. The usual supposedly hilarious crap. His pals laughed harder still, as if they'd never seen anything so funny.

Nobody was laughing when a grim-faced Shane finally emerged from that long meeting. Two security guards had taken up positions outside the closed door before the meeting ended and were ready to guide him out of the building. He was allowed only a few brief moments to collect essential belongings from his desk before being seen to the door. The tension was palpable. Shane wouldn't make eye contact with anyone and no one tried to engage him in conversation. The heavy silence endured even after he was gone. People were in shock at the sudden departure of arguably the most popular salesperson on staff at Brinkley Solutions. Pete even saw one woman dabbing tears from her eyes. She caught him staring and shot him a nasty look, causing Pete to immediately bow his head and stare at the surface of his desk. He did not, however, do this out of embarrassment. Well, not entirely. Maybe a little. Mostly, though, he did it to hide his smile.

Pete hated Shane Watson more than just about anyone else on the planet. It was a hatred that exceeded any ill feelings he harbored toward the truly bad people of the world, including several noted dictators and crooked politicians. He had a more favorable opinion of many of the more well-known serial killers. It wasn't that Pete was a total misanthrope. He genuinely loathed such villainous personages. They were vile and despicable, shoddy excuses for human beings. In his own humble opinion, however, Shane was worse than all of them combined.

The ever-smirking young sales executive's time with the company had lasted just six months, but that had been more than enough time to drive Pete to the brink of utter despair. From day one, the brashly insufferable asshole had made it his mission to torment and humiliate Pete. Watson was an arrogant loudmouth. Pete was humble and soft-spoken. Watson was handsome and athletic. And tall. Pete was considerably shorter and had a slight build. He wasn't genuinely ugly, but no one had ever called him handsome and never would. Watson mocked him for his mediocre looks and introverted nature in merciless fashion, being aggressively mean in a way that should have earned him a pink slip long before his actual dismissal. The problem was that Pete was the man's only object of abuse at the company. Everyone else loved him. They thought he was a great guy. His constant jabs at Pete were seen as being in good fun, a well-meaning way of trying to draw the quieter man out of his shell. If his co-workers noticed Watson's many minor acts of physical abuse against Pete, they either looked the other way or didn't care.

These instances of physical harassment happened multiple times a week. Shane would flick at Pete's ears or smack the back of his head whenever the opportunity to do so arose, which happened with distressing frequency. This was primarily because of the location of Shane's cubicle, which was three down from Pete's own cubicle on the same row. He passed behind Pete several times daily. Every time he went on break or lunch. Every time he retrieved documents from the printer or fax machine. Every time he went to the supervisor's office to ask a question. And he was always careful to abuse Pete when no one was watching. No one who would report him for it, that is.

Pete endured all of it without complaint because, among other reasons, he didn't want to be seen as weak. As a victim. He was a man, not a kid in high school. In theory, he could report the constant abuse to human resources and demand something be done about it. If he had, something probably *would* have been done. In this age of ever-increasing political correctness and sensitivity, maintaining a non-hostile work environment was in the best interests of any company wishing to avoid controversy. As an individual, however, Pete also wished to avoid controversy. He didn't want to be seen as the reason a popular employee was given the boot. The resentment this would foment among his coworkers almost certainly would be more than he could withstand.

He would be forced to quit and find another job. Pete didn't want another job. He liked the one he had. He was good at it. It fit his skill-set. The money was good and the benefits were great. Aside from all that, the prospect of going on a round of job interviews filled him with almost as much dread as one of Watson's slow marches down the aisle between cubicle rows. He just didn't want to do it, so he kept his mouth shut and clung to the desperate hope that he could one day have a heart-to-heart talk with the man and convince him to knock off the abusive behavior. Getting him to stop seemed an unlikely outcome, but he could at least give it a shot. If it worked, great. If it didn't … well, he hadn't yet come up with a plan for next steps, thus the deep depression that had engulfed him over these last several days.

Now, though, he didn't need to come up with a plan, thanks to Shane Watson's abrupt removal from his life. And the best part? He hadn't had to lift a finger to make it happen. For reasons unknown, someone else had done it for him. He didn't even care *why* it had happened. He was sure he would have been consulted beforehand if it'd had anything to do with him. That hadn't happened, though, which meant nobody could blame him for Shane being gone. He was in the clear. He felt liberated. Lighter than air. Free to resume normal life. He felt like throwing open his bedroom window and exclaiming his joy to the world in a loud, jubilant voice.

He didn't do that, of course. Such outbursts just weren't part of the Pete Adler way of doing things. Instead, he got out of bed, stretched and yawned, and strolled out of the bedroom into the hallway with the intent of heading to the kitchen for the day's first cup of coffee.

His house was a small one. The "hallway" was a hallway in name only. It was more of a small, open junction functioning as a means of egress and ingress between the bedroom, bathroom, kitchen, and living room. The kitchen was through the archway in front of him, while the living room was visible through the archway to his right. He was on the brink of stepping through the archway into the kitchen when he abruptly stopped in his tracks, frowned, and thought for a moment about what he had blearily glimpsed in the living room. Or, rather, what he *might* have glimpsed, because surely it couldn't have been real. He was still groggy. His mind was playing tricks on him. That was the only rational explanation. And it was one that made total sense.

Verification nonetheless seemed necessary.

He backtracked a few steps and peered through the archway into the living room. He gasped. His mouth dropped open. If he'd already had a coffee mug in hand, it would have slipped from his fingers and shattered on the floor. He felt weak in the knees. He had to grip the archway frame to keep from falling over. Even with the support of the frame, remaining upright was difficult in those first several moments. During that time, he gaped at the impossible thing in his living room and willed it to go away. He screwed his eyes shut and rapidly repeated the same words several times: "You're not real. Please go away."

At last, he let out a breath and opened his eyes.

"Oh, shit."

She was still there. Denial of this essential point was no longer possible. There was a dead woman on his couch.

TWO

Another few minutes were necessary to gather strength and courage. Pete then tentatively entered the living room, taking a look around to ensure no one else was in there. It was a small space. Behind the TV stand and the large TV atop it was the only nominally viable potential hiding place in the room. A cautious peek into the narrow space behind the stand and the wall revealed only the usual tangle of wires and cables. The back of the couch sat flush against the opposite wall. No one could hide there, unless they were the size of a small cat, which seemed unlikely. This woman hadn't been murdered by some freakish miniature human being. Some big brute had done this heinous thing. A red recliner sat to the left of the couch, away from the wall and turned at an angle to face the TV. He'd seen that no one was behind it upon entering the room, but his paranoia was in overdrive, so he took a closer look. The area behind the recliner was in need of a good sweeping, but there were no lurking villains there, either.

After confirming no one else was in the living room, Pete stood there and stared at the dead woman for a while. He fidgeted. A nervous sweat rose on his brow. His armpits dampened. He made sounds of impotent frustration. Indecision about what to do next threatened to paralyze him. He pictured years passing while he remained rooted to this spot, subsisting on bugs that flew into his mouth while he grew an unruly beard and the hair on his scalp lengthened until it reached the hardwood floor. An absurd notion, of course, but was it really any more ridiculous than the discovery of a murdered woman on his couch?

He didn't think so.

Several minutes passed before the wild jumble of half-formed thoughts raging inside his head settled into something closer to cohesiveness. He then wiped the sweat from his brow and took a reluctant step closer to the couch and the corpse resting upon it. She was in a seated position, with her head tilted backward and her arms splayed out to either side of her. Her legs were crossed. A number of colorful tattoos had been etched into her creamy smooth skin. He was able to see them because most of her flesh was exposed. The dead woman wore only a lacy black bra and black panties. Her feet were ensconced in a pair of black platform heels. She had been an attractive woman, with a slender yet shapely body, large breasts, and a pretty face framed by long locks of hair dyed a shade of black darker than the heart of midnight. The only thing detracting from her beauty were the ugly marks around her neck. She had been brutally strangled prior to being mysteriously deposited here on his couch. A detached part of him noted that at least the killing method employed had been a relatively clean one. If she had been shot or stabbed, blood from her wounds might have leaked onto his couch cushion. It was a callous thing to think in the face of this horror, but that made it no less true.

He didn't know the woman. At this point, that was the only thing he knew for an absolute fact about her inexplicable presence. A woman who looked like this wasn't someone he could have forgotten, even if he'd only glimpsed her in passing. Of all his female acquaintances, not one of them had remotely resembled this gorgeous creature. Some of the ladies he worked with were attractive enough in their own right, but this unfortunate woman had existed in a league far above any of them. She was like a perfect vision out of an erotic dream. Aside from the nasty marks on her neck, that is.

Another thing Pete knew for an absolute fact was that he was not responsible for this woman's death. His hands had not created those hideous bruises on her crushed throat. Even if he'd ever felt inclined to do such an awful thing, he doubted he was physically capable of it. A much stronger person had done this. Someone with bigger hands. Someone able to firmly hold the woman in place without any real trouble while committing this vile act.

And yet the question remained, how was it she had come to be here on his couch?

He was a sound sleeper most nights, but he had a hard time believing an intruder could have broken into his house and dumped a corpse on his couch without awakening him. Aside from that, he rarely neglected to arm his alarm system before going to bed at night. He clearly remembered doing so last night. In fact, he hadn't yet disarmed it, as he always did shortly after waking each day. His eyes widened at this thought and in another moment he spun about, racing out of the living room and into the kitchen. The alarm system's keypad was mounted on the wall just inside the archway.

The system was still armed. This gave rise to a fresh slew of troubling questions. The only explanation was that someone had somehow entered his house without setting off the alarm and had then temporarily disarmed the system before resetting it. He could make no sense of the notion. Only someone with a key to his house and knowledge of the alarm code could have done such a thing. Unless, of course, the perpetrator was some kind of master thief straight out of a Hollywood heist movie. This was another thing that fell into the category of the highly unlikely. Then again, there wasn't a lot to work with in the realm of more realistic scenarios, either. The only keys to his house were his own. He knew this because he'd changed out the locks shortly after moving in and had not opted to have duplicate keys made. Nor had he ever shared his alarm code with anyone. There was no one he trusted enough for that.

Pete frowned as he scratched the side of his head. Unless he was somehow missing something obvious and crucial, there was no way an intruder could have gotten into his house last night without him knowing about it. And yet that was exactly what seemed to have happened. It was a conundrum. There was a missing puzzle piece he didn't know about. All he had to do was identify what that was and the whole mystery would unravel.

Easier said than done, but he had to try.

The first step in that process, he decided, was to definitively rule out a break-in. He did a quick tour of every room in the house in search of any signs of forced entry. There was nothing. All the windows were locked down tight the way they always were. There were no marks in the wood indicating that anyone had tried to jimmy their way in. He was also belatedly able to rule out the possibility of a fiend lurking in some other part of the house, which was a massive relief in one way. In another way, it only further deepened the mystery.

He reentered the living room in a daze, mind reeling as he struggled to figure out what had happened. Although the idea of someone having forced their way into his home was a disturbing one, he almost wished he'd discovered evidence to support the possibility. At least it would have been something he could make sense of and wrap his head around. As far as he was concerned, the lack of an obvious explanation for the dead woman's presence here was far more disturbing than the reality of the corpse itself. He tried forcing his mind in directions beyond the obvious. This soon caused him to examine the situation from a perspective that at first struck him as absurd, but it was one he was forced to consider because it was the only thing that fit the available evidence.

The question Pete Adler was forced to ask himself was this—was he, after all, the person behind this woman's murder? It would account for the absence of break-in evidence and the mystery of the alarm system.

The idea made no sense on any level. He wasn't a violent man and never had been. Though he'd had decidedly mixed luck with women on the romantic front most of his life, he'd never harbored hatred in his heart for the opposite gender. He respected them. He simply couldn't imagine himself doing something so vile as murdering an innocent woman, not even in the midst of some kind of blackout or psychotic fugue state. Again, though, this was unlikely in the extreme. He was mentally stable. Always had been. He drank only in moderation. Last night he didn't have so much as a single drop of alcohol. Not only that, but he clearly remembered crawling into bed, turning off his bedside lamp, and slowly drifting off to sleep. This morning he woke up feeling physically and mentally refreshed, the way he always did after a good night's solid sleep. This seemed to rule out the outlandish notion that he'd suffered some kind of bizarre psychotic break in the middle of the night and gone out prowling somewhere for a victim. Not that he'd seriously believed it possible in the first place. Given the circumstances, the possibility had merited consideration. Well, he'd considered it, and now he was rejecting it out of hand.

Which brought him back to square one. He had a dead woman in his house. A *murdered* woman. And not even the merest *hint* yet of why or how this had happened.

He heaved a breath and shook his head in consternation. "Goddammit."

And now he was faced with a new question.

What next?

He couldn't just stand here and fret over the situation forever. He'd already established he wasn't in any immediate personal danger. The perpetrator, whoever he or she had been, was gone. Unless, maybe, the person was hanging around somewhere outside, waiting to see what happened next. He did another quick tour of the house, peeking out windows in search of lurking creeps, but didn't see anybody. Back in the living room, he returned to the question of what to do next. He knew what the police would expect of him. They would expect him to report discovering the corpse. In the eyes of the law, he should be calling 911 right now. His phone was on the nightstand next to his bed. He thought about going back to the bedroom to retrieve it, but his feet didn't seem inclined to turn in that direction, at least not yet.

The big reason for his hesitation was the issue of culpability. If he summoned the police, they would inspect the scene and ask many of the questions he'd asked himself. He had a sick feeling he would immediately be pegged as the prime suspect in the woman's death, because who else could have done it?

Though every instinct he had rebelled against the idea, he moved a few steps closer to the dead woman, almost close enough to reach out and touch her, though he refrained from doing that. Up close, those marks were even uglier. The killer's grip had crushed her throat. Pete leaned in closer still, tilting his head side to side to examine the marks. He saw what looked to him like thumbnail indentations on the underside of her chin. Pete, of course, had no real forensic expertise, but it looked to him as if the killer had strangled the woman with his bare hands. This was good news. Despite the tragic element of the situation, he couldn't help smiling. It seemed likely some of the killer's DNA was embedded in the woman's skin. The police might initially suspect him, but ultimately the physical evidence would absolve him of involvement in the crime. The rest of it might remain inexplicable for some time to come, but the thing about DNA was that it didn't lie. He was fortunate he'd thus far refrained from touching the woman and thereby leaving traces of his own DNA on her body. At that point, his smile began to slip as he thought about the way he was leaning over her. He then thought about true crime and cop shows he'd seen, in particular the ones in which people were convicted of heinous murders on the basis of a single stray strand of hair recovered from the scene. A strand of his own hair might already have fallen on this woman.

Pete let out a yelp of alarm and jumped back. He bumped into the coffee table, causing it to skid backward. And that was when he saw it—the item that had been hidden beneath the table.

A woman's black handbag.

THREE

There was little doubt the expensive-looking handbag had belonged to the dead woman. Many months had passed since he'd last had a female guest in his home. The last one had been Mary Wilson, a girl from work he'd dated a handful of times. He'd been unsurprised when she decided she wasn't interested and broke it off with him. Romantic failure was, after all, one of the big recurring themes in his life. By this point, he was certain he would never get married or have a chance to start a family. For the most part, he felt accepting of this fate. It was just his unfortunate lot in life. Things could be worse. He had his health. A roof over his head. A decent income. He'd liked Mary, though, and a little part of him still experienced pangs of regret when he thought about her, which was more frequently than he would have wished, given that he still saw her at work every day.

He approached the couch again and knelt in front of the handbag. There was zero chance the bag was something left behind by Mary. For one thing, he would have noticed it resting there beneath the coffee table at some point in the intervening months. For another, if Mary *had* left the bag here, she would have asked him to bring it to work and return it to her. There was also the fact that he'd pulled the table aside to sweep beneath it countless times since then. No, *this* bag had absolutely belonged to the corpse on his couch, which meant her wallet was likely inside it, unless the killer had taken it with him (or her, he immediately amended again, though he seriously doubted a woman had committed this brutal act). If the wallet hadn't been taken, it almost certainly contained the murdered woman's driver's license and possibly numerous other identifying items.

Aside from the essential fact of the dead woman's presence, perhaps the most frustrating thing about the situation for Pete was his lack of knowledge about … well, every goddamn aspect of it, pretty much. Answers to the bigger questions—the identity of the murderer, for instance, and the how and why of the victim being deposited on his couch—remained frustratingly out of reach. There was now, however, a good chance he could at least attach a name to the corpse. All he had to do was reach into the purse, extract the wallet, and examine its contents.

Except that he couldn't. The reason was the same one that had nearly caused him to fall over the coffee table moments ago. By putting his hands all over a murdered woman's belongings, he would thoroughly contaminate them with his DNA, thereby contributing to the evidence against him.

"Shit."

Leaving the bag undisturbed, he got to his feet and began to restlessly pace about the small open part of the living room. He mumbled to himself and ran his hands through his hair—making an unruly mess of it—as he resumed the thus far fruitless attempt to reason out what had happened here. This process continued for another frustrating several minutes, until he again accepted the hopelessness of arriving at a solution with the evidence at hand. He didn't have the skills for this. He wasn't a cop or a private investigator. This was a job for professionals.

"Fuck it."

He went into his bedroom to get his phone, which was right where he'd left it before going to sleep last night, at the edge of his nightstand near the base of the lamp. Snatching it up, he hurried back out to the living room, where he tapped the phone icon on the screen and prepared to punch in 9-1-1. He'd firmly made up his mind. Getting the police involved was scary, but it had to happen. He was in over his head. It was time to bite the bullet and take the hard first step of putting this nightmare behind him. He tapped the '9' button and the number appeared at the top of the screen. His forefinger then immediately moved to the '1' button ... where it hesitated, hovering above the screen.

Pete frowned.

The hesitation was not another case of his nerves getting the better of him. It was instead rooted in something he'd glimpsed obliquely while in the bedroom, a little something off that hadn't registered until just now. He hadn't noticed it upon awakening and crawling out of bed, but he'd still been a bit groggy at the time, so that was understandable. He'd even missed it when searching for signs of a break-in. Now, however, he was fully awake, alert, not so focused on the doors and windows, and he'd still almost missed it.

Feeling almost numb with dread, he returned to the bedroom, moved to the side of the bed, and stared down. He swallowed with difficulty when he saw the thing he'd glimpsed moments ago. It was easy to see why he'd missed it. Not much of it was visible. Only a tiny bit of sheer black fabric peeked out from beneath the bedspread on the side of the bed opposite of where he always slept. Leaning over the bed, he pulled the bedspread back and groaned when he saw the rest of the flimsy, lacy garment. It was a tiny negligee. He could only surmise that it had belonged to the dead woman, but what was it doing in his bed? He'd gone to bed alone last night. This was indisputable fact as far as he was concerned and something already covered in his mental review of the previous evening, which had been nothing more than a quiet and unremarkable night alone at home. There were no holes in his memory of the evening, at least that portion of it for which he had been awake.

He could only conclude someone had come into his room and slipped the little scrap of sheer fabric underneath his bedspread without waking him, a person who could only have been the dead woman's killer. It seemed like such a bizarre and pointless thing to do, every bit as inexplicable as the presence of the corpse in his living room. He couldn't understand why a murderer would dispose of a victim's body in a random person's home rather than in a more standard way, such as dumping it in a ravine or some other remote, rural location. Unless the killer was some kind of macabre prankster. Or unless ...

Pete frowned.

Could this possibly be part of an orchestrated effort to frame him for the woman's murder?

His first instinct was to scoff at the idea. He could think of no good reason anyone would do this terrible thing to him. He mulled it over a moment longer and frowned, realizing that might not be entirely accurate. An image of a stunned-looking Shane Watson being escorted out of the building yesterday came to him then. Pete didn't know the details yet, but it was clear Watson had been abruptly terminated from his position with the company. He'd been unceremoniously given the boot, not just warned or put on probation, as was the usual way of things when the company had issues with an employee. Whatever the reason for his dismissal, it had to have been something serious. Criminal-level serious, possibly.

Pete could see that being the case. So what, though? If something like that was the reason for Watson's firing, what did it have to do with him?

Not a damn thing, that's what.

Then again, there was a chance his guess was way off the mark. Maybe Watson's firing *did* have something to do with the man's abusive treatment of him. Perhaps it had been a mere contributing factor rather than the primary reason. That seemed plausible. Pete had never reported the behavior, but maybe some well-meaning third party had done so on his behalf. In that case, Watson might still hold it against him if the issue had been brought up during that closed-door meeting. Pete then might have become a convenient target for his rage. Watson couldn't strike back against Brinkley Solutions in any meaningful way, but he *could* lash out at a meek little former coworker.

A low whimper emerged through Pete's tightly clenched teeth.

He thought about Shane Watson's size. In particular, those big hands. The hands of a brute. The man was big and strong enough to have strangled the dead woman with his bare hands. His constant acts of aggression against Pete suggested he had the temperament to commit such an act.

There was a thread of real logic to all of this, the first hint of it he'd encountered since discovering the body in his living room. He had identified a possible motive and a suspect capable of perpetrating the act. Still eluding him was an answer to the question of how the man had gotten into his house without forcing his way in or tripping the alarm.

He was still desperately trying to figure that part of it out when he heard the strident knock on his front door.

FOUR

Pete yelped in surprise when he heard the knock. The shock of hearing the sound was exacerbated by the bizarre situation confronting him this morning, but he would have been startled by the intrusion even on a normal weekend morning. Unexpected knocks on his door were a rare thing. He had a large and aggressively worded sign warning off solicitors mounted inside the screen door. It had proven quite effective over the years. On extremely rare occasions, especially dense and oblivious people ignored the sign and knocked, but this was the first time it had happened in almost a year.

The knock came again, louder and more strident this time.

Pete sat on the edge of his bed, deciding he would wait right there until the unknown caller gave up and went away. It would happen sooner or later, unless the person knocking was a thief checking for unoccupied homes. The knocking might be a pre-cursor to kicking the door open and making a quick snatch and grab of something valuable before the police could arrive. Think-ing about it made him smile. If that happened, the intruder would get a hell of a shock shortly after bursting inside. He pic-tured the thief screaming at the sight of the dead body and run-ning out of the house without any loot.

He was chuckling at this image when he heard a faint voice calling out to him from the porch. The smile froze on his face, slowly giving way to a frown. There were a couple of strange things about what he was hearing. Though the sound was faint, he could tell the person on his porch was a woman. He hadn't had a female visitor since his last date with Mary Wilson, many months ago. The second strange thing was that whoever it was knew his name.

The knocking and yelling got louder. The deep state of agita-tion evident in the woman's voice was worrisome. She was mak-ing enough noise to attract attention from neighbors. Maybe enough to prompt one of them to pick up a phone and call the police. And having the cops show up at this stage of things was the last thing he wanted. It had taken this unexpected intrusion for him to fully realize this. He didn't want to talk to the police about this until he was calmer and had rehearsed a speech de-signed to highlight the impossibility of him having anything to do with the woman's death. And maybe not even then, because a new idea was occurring to him, one that was questionable from a moral standpoint and absolutely a thing that would cause the cops to view him in a decidedly less than favorable light.

If they found out about it, that is.

The presence of the body in his house was the big issue. The simplest way out of the current dilemma was obvious. All he had to do was remove the body from the premises. Problem solved. Many troubling questions would remain, of course, but in his pantry was a box of big black trash bags. He could wrap the corpse up in some of those, wait until nightfall, and, when he was as sure as he could be that no one was watching, carry her out to his car, stash her in the trunk, and drive out of the city to some remote rural location to dump her. In a way, it would be a shitty thing to do. She had been a human being. A person with real feelings and hopes and dreams, with loved ones who cared about her. Dumping her somewhere like a load of trash would be a reprehensible gesture of disrespect for her basic humanity and the person she had been. This was undeniably true and Pete hated that aspect of it, but there was a powerful allure in the possibility of a relatively clean solution to his problem. Yes, she had been a human being. It sucked that someone had killed her. Pete hadn't known her, though, and all she was to him was a pile of highly inconvenient dead meat.

A tentative feeling of relief came over him at knowing he'd settled on a course of action. He felt lighter now, as if a burden had been removed. To a degree, it was an illusory feeling. The problem was still very much with him and would be until he was rid of the corpse many hours from now, but he embraced the feeling anyway. His plan was one of avoidance. It meant he wouldn't have to face the cops and their questions. Knowing this added to his sense of relief.

Meanwhile, the banging on his door had only intensified.

"Dammit."

Pete got up and walked out of the bedroom. Once he was out in the living room, he could hear the woman's voice more clearly. It sounded familiar. She was still repeatedly calling out his name. He frowned as he tentatively approached the door, where he lifted one of the blind slats covering the window and peeked out at the woman on the porch. His frown deepened when he saw who she was. He couldn't imagine why Mary Wilson had decided to pay him an unannounced visit after so many months. She had made her lack of interest in him quite clear after that last date. Though their subsequent interactions at work had been civil enough, there was always an underlying chill in her voice every time she was forced to converse with him. There had never been the slightest doubt in his mind that she was out of his life permanently on a non-professional level.

And yet here she was.

As puzzling as this was, her demeanor was an even bigger mystery. He had never seen her so visibly upset about anything. She was always calm. Even when she'd cut things off with him, she'd done so in a nearly emotionless way. Well, she was anything but calm and emotionless now. Seeing the obvious strain in her expression was almost like looking into the face of a stranger.

She stopped yelling and banging on the door the instant he

peeked out at her. Though he'd been careful to lift the blind slat only a tiny fraction of an inch, he knew it'd been enough to make his presence known, a guess confirmed by her next words.

She sighed heavily and spoke in a calmer tone, although still loudly enough to be heard through the door. "I can see you looking out at me, Pete. Please open the door so we can talk. It's important."

Pete glanced over at the dead woman before replying. Peeking through the blind slat again, he cleared his throat and raised his voice. "Just a minute. I, uh ... just woke up. Let me put on some clothes."

The look on her face was not a happy one. "Hurry, please. Trust me, you need to know about this. You might be in danger."

Pete frowned. "In danger? From who? Or what?"

She rolled her eyes in exasperation. "Open the door and I'll tell you."

"Yeah, okay. Just give me a minute."

He let the blind slat slide back into place and backed away from the door before she could say anything else. Panic and indecision again threatened to paralyze him. Here was another seemingly impossible situation. Mary was clearly determined to see him. Persuading her to go away seemed unlikely. He could claim he'd come down with something contagious and didn't want to risk giving it to her by opening the door, but he doubted she'd buy the excuse. The only thing he could think to do was open the door and talk to her without allowing her inside. He would have to take the preemptive step of barging his way out onto the porch and closing the screen door behind him. Otherwise, he knew, she would push her way past him and enter the house uninvited. She was too assertive that way. Giving her even an inch would be dangerous.

Pete flinched when she banged on the door again. He belatedly realized more than a full minute had passed.

She called out to him again, voice raised higher this time. "Is something wrong in there, Pete? I'm very worried about you. If you don't open up soon, I may have to call the police."

Pete winced.

Oh, shit.

He couldn't fathom what could have Mary worried enough to summon the police here. Okay, yes, he was embroiled in an undeniably serious situation. Someone had been murdered. The killer had come into his house. These were things that would prompt concern in anyone who cared about him, *if* they knew about them. Mary, however, couldn't possibly know there was a murdered woman in his house. This fact alone made the level of concern she was displaying difficult to understand. Short of murder—or the threat of murder—what could have her so upset? And why was she concerned at all? Until just now, he had been convinced she didn't give a damn about his well-being one way or the other.

He ran a hand through his hair and made a sound that was part laugh and part whimper.

What the fuck is going on here?

26

She banged on the door yet again.

"Seriously, Pete, open the fuck up! I'm getting out my phone. I'm calling 911 right now."

"*Stop!*"

The ferocity in his own voice surprised Pete. There was an unmistakable desperation in the sound, a factor that might prompt her to dial 911 even more quickly. He started shaking. It was only moments ago that he'd felt such relief at deciding to leave the cops out of this thing. Now Mary was on the verge of making it an issue again. He was starting to feel as if everybody and everything in the universe was conspiring against him.

He had to find a way to calm her down and buy some time. Pete sucked in a big breath and blew it out. He moved closer to the door and resumed speaking in a calmer but still forceful tone. "Mary, do not call 911. I promise you I'm okay. I'll open the door in just another minute or two, I swear."

A silent moment elapsed.

Then Mary said, "Okay, Pete. But another minute or two is all you get."

He again backed away from the door and looked at the beautiful dead woman on the couch. Inspiration struck. It was a crazy notion, but he recognized right away it was something he had to do. Not opening the door within the next couple minutes wasn't an option. He was positive Mary would follow through on her threat to call 911 if he didn't. Unfortunately, opening the door came with other risks. His intent to barge his way out there and close the door behind him was all well and good, but there was a chance Mary might move faster than he could and push her way into the house. Even the slimmest chance of that was more than he was willing to risk.

Something had to be done about the dead woman. Right now. There wasn't time to drag her out of the living room and stuff the corpse under his bed or in a closet. But there might be just enough time to get creative and possibly arrange things in a way that conveyed a false—and less damning—impression.

He went to the hallway closet and pulled the door open, grabbing a blanket from the stack of them on the middle shelf. Next he grabbed a pillow from his bedroom and raced back out to the living room, where he set these items on the coffee table and psyched himself up to do the unpleasant thing that needed doing.

Doing this meant abandoning any lingering concerns about contaminating the corpse with his DNA. This was the point of no return as far as being able to opt for a more rational course of action. It meant an absolute, unbreakable commitment to breaking the law. There was no time to think about it any further. He had to act now or resign himself to dealing with the cops after Mary made that call. On a detached level, he was dimly aware of resentment stirring within him, a bitterness at Mary for meddling in his business at this most inconvenient of times. He shoved the feeling down deep inside, made it something he could either deal with later or forget forever, depending on how things worked out.

He took hold of the dead woman by her ankles and stretched

out her legs. The corpse was surprisingly pliable. Until this morning, his limited knowledge of the postmortem reality of dead human bodies had been gleaned entirely from movies and TV shows. There was none of the stiffness he'd expected to encounter, which allowed him to manipulate the body without much difficulty. This was a lucky break. He wouldn't have to force the body into the desired position. As he worked to get the body arranged the way he wanted it, however, he couldn't help reflecting on the more disturbing implications of its current condition. She wasn't stinking yet and rigor mortis had not yet had time to set in. And she was still warm. All of which meant she must have died a very short while ago, perhaps not long at all before he woke up. The sun might already have risen by then. It made him realize how narrowly he might have missed a confrontation with the killer, a thought that made him shudder.

After getting the dead woman stretched out on the couch, he turned her so she was facing the back of it. This required reaching beneath the torso and getting a good grip on it before heaving the body over. Handling the corpse in so intimate a way triggered a primal revulsion, making his stomach flutter. It was an instinct possessed by most of the living, he knew, this need to flinch away from the physical reality of death, but he didn't have the luxury of doing that right now. He removed the woman's platform heels and set them on the floor next to her purse. Then he slid a pillow under her head and spread the blanket over her unmoving form, taking care to pull it up high and cover her bruised neck. After that, one last subtle adjustment, turning her head so her face would be almost completely out of sight to a casual observer. You wouldn't be able to tell she wasn't breathing unless you leaned over her and checked, which Mary had no reason to do.

Pete stepped back a bit to observe his handiwork. He thought the body's position on the couch looked naturalistic. She looked like she was curled up in a semi-fetal position, with her knees bent slightly and her arms tucked in against her stomach.

He sighed. It would have to be good enough.

The whole process had taken less than five minutes. He knew this from the clock on the cable box. Unfortunately, the time elapsed was still more than double the time allotted him by Mary, who still hadn't piped up again. This might all have been for nothing. The cops might already be on their way.

There was nothing he could do about that now.

He'd done this thing and there was no taking it back.

After a quick dash into the kitchen to disarm the alarm system, he went to the front door and opened it.

FIVE

"**I**t's about fucking time."

These were the first words out of Mary's mouth as he opened the door and started to step outside. She put a hand against his chest and pushed him back inside, closing the door behind her as she followed him into the house.

Pete's hands curled into fists at his sides, an instinctive effort to keep himself from shaking. The last thing he needed was for her to see how deeply rattled he was feeling. He considered trying out a phony smile, but he figured the strain in the expression would be immediately obvious. His heart pounded. Sweat formed in his armpits. He could only hope more sweat didn't start pouring down his forehead.

"Sorry to barge in this way, Pete, but—"

She stopped talking the instant she realized someone else was in the room with them. A corpse instead of another living person, but she wouldn't know that. Or so he hoped. If she somehow intuited the nameless woman's status as one of the deceased, he didn't know what he'd do at that point.

Break down crying, probably.

Her head swiveled slowly toward the couch. She gave the unmoving form beneath the blanket a prolonged moment of silent appraisal. There was a smile on her lips when she again looked at Pete. It was a smile with a bit of a smirk in it. "I'm sorry, Pete, I didn't realize you had company."

He chuckled softly and ran a hand through his hair, one of his most telling nervous habits. He always did that when he was feeling anxious. Mary knew it, too. Hopefully in this case she would interpret it as embarrassment at having been caught with a comely female guest by his ex.

"I, uh, yeah. Yeah, she's, uh ... asleep."

Mary's expression became more smirk than smile. "I see that." Her gaze flicked to the floor, an eyebrow arching when she saw the handbag and platform heels. She looked at Pete and smiled. "Nice shoes."

Pete nodded. He ran a hand through his hair.

Dammit.

"Yeah."

He couldn't think of anything else to say.

Such was not the case for Mary. "They look like the kind of shoes a certain type of professional woman would wear." There was a playful glint in her eyes. "A dominatrix, perhaps. Or maybe an exotic dancer."

Pete frowned. "What?"

"Your friend wouldn't happen to be a stripper, would she?"

Pete shook his head. "Of course not."

The denial came instantly to his lips, but only because the possibility hadn't occurred to him. He didn't hang out in strip clubs and didn't know any women who took their clothes off for a living. It just wasn't a part of his world. But maybe Mary was right.

Mary gave him a cockeyed look, tilting her head slightly. "Hmm."

Anxious to push the conversation in a different direction, Pete coughed and cleared his throat. "Look, can we take this to the kitchen? I don't want to wake my friend. We had kind of a wild night, maybe drank a bit too much. Maybe a *lot* too much. I'm trying to let her sleep it off."

Mary's expression was one of blatant disbelief. "My, my, Pete. I didn't know you had nights like that. They certainly never happened when we were dating."

His face reddened. "Um ..."

Mary laughed and indicated the archway behind him with a tilt of her chin. "Relax, Pete. I'm just giving you shit. It's good to see you loosening up some. By all means, let's take this to the kitchen."

Pete nodded and led the way.

Once they were seated at the small table in the kitchen, Pete began to feel even more flustered as he belatedly took note of some of the things he'd always found attractive about Mary. The full lips. The artful way she applied her eye makeup, making her green eyes look big and expressive. Her pinned-up long blonde hair, worn in a way that made him think of actresses from a by-gone era. It was Saturday, but she looked as if she were still dressed for work, wearing a beige pencil skirt that reached her knees and a pinstriped top. As always, she managed to make the somewhat conservative attire look sexy.

They had been sitting there close to a full minute when Pete realized she was just smiling at him and not saying anything. "Um, can I get you a drink or something?"

She arched an eyebrow. "Awfully early in the day for a drink."

"I didn't mean booze." Pete frowned as he remembered the lie he'd told about his fictional wild night with the dead woman. "Besides, another drink is the last thing I need right now. But I could get you a water or something. Maybe put on a pot of cof-fee."

She shook her head. "No need for that. It's funny, though. You don't have that morning-after-a-bender look. In fact, you look sort of bright-eyed and bushy-tailed. As if you had a solid night of sleep."

Pete's guts started twisting up again at these words. She was barely making any effort to hide her skepticism regarding his supposed wild night. He again endeavored to steer the conversation in another direction. "You said you had something urgent to tell me. A matter of life and death from the sound of it. What could possibly have you so worried that you were on the verge of calling the cops?"

"I overheard something last night. Part of a conversation I wasn't meant to hear. I didn't take it seriously at first, but I got to thinking about it this morning and started to get scared. I decided I needed to warn you."

Pete shifted in his chair, frowning again. His only concern up to this point had been humoring Mary long enough to allay whatever fears she had and send her on her way. Now, though, his curiosity was genuinely piqued. "And this conversation you overheard had something to do with me?"

"That's right. By the way, I apologize for all the noise I made at your door. I was just desperate to get your attention." A corner of her mouth twitched, that smirk threatening to make a return. "It's amazing your friend managed to sleep through all that."

Pete opted to ignore that last remark. "Where did this conversation take place?"

Mary had set her purse on the table. She drew it closer now and took out a pack of cigarettes and a cheap plastic lighter. "You don't mind if I smoke."

The way she said it was more like a statement than a question. Pete wasn't a smoker and in general didn't like for others to smoke in his house, but he'd made an exception for Mary when he'd been dating her. Desperation for sex had a way of causing a guy to at least temporarily suspend his usual rules. He'd done everything he could to smooth that potential path to the bedroom. She never did sleep with him, though, and the smell of cigarette smoke had lingered in the house for months afterward. It seemed he was still harboring a trace of bitterness in the matter, because he was tempted to be petty and deny her smoking privileges.

Instead, he got up from the table and opened a cupboard above the sink and took down a package of red plastic drinking cups. He tore the plastic open, took out one of the cups, and returned the package to the cupboard. At the sink, he turned on the cold water tap and put about a half inch of water in the cup. He set the cup on the table and sat down again.

Mary made a tsk-tsk sound and shook her head as she tapped a cigarette out of the pack. "All these months later, Pete, and you still don't have a proper ashtray?"

He shrugged. "It was never an issue again until today."

She grunted, flicking the lighter and applying the flame to the tip of the cigarette. "Nevertheless, a man should be prepared for any situation. That's what my father always told me. Any proper household should have at least one ashtray on hand for guests."

"Well, I don't. I guess I'm not the man your father was."

Mary leaned back slightly in her chair and blew a cloud of smoke at the ceiling. "You can say that again."

Pete sighed. "I'm beginning to suspect the real reason you're here is just to mess with me. Are you going to tell me about this conversation you supposedly overheard or not?"

Mary took another, shorter drag on the cigarette, exhaling more smoke. This time it drifted across the table toward Pete.

"Gosh, you were never this short with me when we were dating." She laughed when she saw his look of consternation. "Hey, I get it. You wanted to fuck me and were on your best behavior. Who knows, maybe you would have gotten somewhere if you'd been more like the guy I'm seeing today. Someone who stands up for himself, I mean."

Pete shifted again in his chair, becoming steadily more agitated the longer she avoided the supposed reason behind her visit. "I stand up for myself."

She laughed with more vigor than before, tossing her head back as the sound rolled out of her. The hearty laughter made her breasts move beneath the pinstriped top in a way Pete found distracting despite his overriding desire for her to finally get to the point and make a quicker exit from his house.

"Like the way you've been standing up to Shane Watson all these months, you mean?"

Pete felt a fresh touch of heat in his cheeks. He tugged at the collar of his T-shirt. The armpits of the shirt were becoming damp again. His discomfort wasn't just his anxiety over the concealed dead body in his living room. The whole Shane Watson thing filled him with shame. He didn't like being seen as weak and unmanly in the eyes of an attractive woman, even if that impression was nothing less than the absolute truth.

"I don't know what you're talking about."

Mary rolled her eyes. "Come on, Pete. Everyone knew what was going on. We saw how he treated you, like a big playground bully picking on a scrawny wimp. I'm just sorry none of us ever did anything about it."

Pete said nothing to that. He just sat there and stared at her, silently willing her to get on with it.

Mary puffed more smoke at the ceiling. "I know you're getting annoyed with me. I can see it in your eyes. But this is actually relevant to why I'm here. That conversation I overheard last night? It was between Shane and the guy who was his best buddy at work. Jake Edgerton. You know him, right?"

A feeling of apprehension came over Pete at hearing that name. He did know Edgerton, unfortunately. Shane and Jake Edgerton were cut from the same mold. Edgerton was as handsome as Shane and nearly as obnoxious. He smirked and snickered along with Shane whenever Pete had the misfortune of getting anywhere near them. Though he didn't engage in any direct physical abuse the way his friend did, Pete had always sensed it was only because the man had a slightly more developed sense of self-preservation. He was willing to go right up to the line in terms of acceptable workplace behavior. Unlike his friend, however, he never quite completely crossed that line.

"I know him, yeah," Pete said, his tone more subdued than before. "What were they saying about me? And where the hell was this?"

Mary tapped ash into the plastic cup. "A bunch of us got to talking after work. Everyone was upset about what happened to Shane. We decided to meet up for drinks over at La Mesa. You know the place?"

La Mesa was a Mexican restaurant. He'd been there exactly

one time, several months ago. With Mary. Who apparently hadn't found the occasion memorable. No surprise there.

"I know it."

"You should go sometime. They have awesome margaritas."

Pete grunted. "I'll keep it in mind."

Mary dropped her half-smoked cigarette in the plastic cup. There was a faint fizzle as the lit tip hit the water at the bottom. She leaned back in her chair again and folded her hands primly in her lap. "Someone called Shane and invited him. We all thought he'd be too embarrassed about being fired and wouldn't show up, but he did. He was in kind of a surly mood, as you might imagine, but all the girls tried to make him feel better and it seemed to work. He had some drinks and started to loosen up. We were there for hours. Everybody was joking and having a grand time. Jake showed up at some point. Things started getting blurry after a while. I kept having to go out to the patio to grab a smoke. Jake and Shane were sort of huddled together the last time I went out there. It was obvious they were trying to talk privately. I couldn't hear what they were saying, but the anger in their voices came through loud and clear."

Pete's heart started beating a little faster again. "And they were talking about me?"

Mary lifted one shoulder in a little half-shrug. "I couldn't hear what they were talking about at first. Too much noise. That little patio is right outside the bar. I was feeling a little mischievous after six or seven of those giant margaritas and decided to creep up on them and eavesdrop." Her expression darkened noticeably, every trace of the mirth that had been there fading away. "If I'd known what I was about to hear, I would have stayed away. Because it was scary, Pete. Really, really scary. Later on, I just felt lucky they didn't seem to notice me. And, yes, they were talking about you. Shane was convinced you had something to do with his firing. They were hatching a plan to get back at you. And I don't mean some harmless little prank."

Pete couldn't help thinking about the corpse in his living room. If Mary was telling the truth—and he was inclined to believe her at this point—the dead woman had to be a part of Shane's revenge plot. The body showing up in his house the morning after Mary had heard those two assholes conspiring against him couldn't just be coincidence.

"What else did they say?"

Mary picked up her cigarette pack and tapped it in a seemingly nervous way against the table. "Shane wanted to kill you. I heard him say that. My heart almost stopped, Pete. I couldn't believe what I was hearing. I wanted to run and hide before they could notice me, but it was like I was paralyzed. They were both so drunk, though. Drunk and oblivious. They just kept running their mouths about how they wanted to hurt you. Shane seemed to decide killing you the same day he got fired might not be such a good idea. He'd be a suspect, seeing as how the way he treated you at work was brought up as a factor in his termination meeting. He wanted to do something sneakier. Maybe get you in trouble somehow."

Pete got up from the table and started pacing about the little kitchen. He ran a hand through his hair and made anxious little huffing noises. Hiding his anxiety from Mary was something he no longer cared about. She didn't know the woman on his couch was dead and would believe his fretful behavior stemmed solely from what she had told him. In reality, it was the combination of those things that had him feeling like he was ready to crawl out of his skin. An impulse to come clean with Mary and tell her about the dead woman flitted through his head. He was terrified of what might happen in the wake of the revelation, but there would also be relief in telling someone about it. Given the things she'd overheard last night, it couldn't come as a complete shock. Mary remained where she was as he continued to pace and think about it, eyeing him in a curious way from her seat at the table as she took another cigarette from the pack.

He was within seconds of blurting it all out when he thought of something that made him abruptly cease pacing and direct a frowning look at Mary. "If you were this worried about me last night, why did you wait until now to warn me about it? And why come to my house? Why not just text or call me?"

Mary sighed and held the unlit cigarette pinched between her fingers. "I guess I was in a state of shock. Not a good combination with drunkenness. I got out of there and called an Uber to take me home. I told myself what I'd heard was just drunk talk. That they'd forget that foolishness when they woke up the next day."

Pete returned to his seat at the table. He eyed the pack of cigarettes and considered asking for one. Maybe they'd help with his nerves. Probably not, though. That probably only worked for people who were already regular smokers. "But you reconsidered this morning, apparently."

She nodded and belatedly lit the second cigarette. "I did. And I came to your house because ... well, because I no longer had your number stored in my phone. I deleted it after ... well, you know."

Pete did know.

He had no desire to take even one more step down that conversational path, though. The uncomfortable subject of his brief dating history with Mary belonged in the past. He still found her incredibly attractive, which made the situation all the more uncomfortable. The sooner she was out of his house, the better.

He stood up again and pushed the chair he'd been sitting in under the table. "Well, thanks for letting me know about this. I'll take it under advisement and figure out what to do."

Mary puffed smoke and raised an eyebrow. "Is that my cue to leave?"

Pete sighed. "I'm sorry. I don't mean to rush you. It's just that I just got up and, well ..." He directed a meaningful glance in the direction of the hallway. Mary gave him another of her quietly curious looks and waited for him to elaborate. He'd hoped she'd just take the hint and go. She appeared in need of an extra nudge, however. "My friend will probably be waking up soon. I'd rather there not be anyone else here when that happens."

Mary took a long draw off her cigarette, holding the smoke in for several seconds before softly exhaling another white cloud that drifted slowly toward Pete. The second cigarette followed the first into the plastic cup. There was another soft fizzle as it hit the wet bottom. Pete couldn't help noting she'd again only smoked half a cigarette. He wondered if it was her way of trying to cut back. He was almost curious enough to ask her about it, but he held his tongue, not wishing to give her even the slightest excuse to draw things out and keep talking.

She looked him in the eye and held his gaze for another long-ish moment, her expression devoid of the smirking playfulness that had been there throughout their conversation. At last, she got to her feet and took her time smoothing out her skirt. She then grabbed her little purse and tucked it under an arm. "You need to take this situation seriously, Pete. Hopefully Shane will reconsider doing anything stupid once he's sobered up, but you should keep your guard up for a while. Stay aware of your surroundings when you go out. Keep that alarm on when you're at home."

Pete forced a smile. "I will. And, uh, thanks for the concern."

Mary smiled. "No problem. I do still care, believe it or not." She brushed past him and approached the alarm keypad, glancing back at him with that smile still in place. "In fact, I'll just go ahead and take care of this now in case you forget."

Pete's smile faltered as he watched her punch in his alarm code. "Um ..."

She stepped back from the keypad as it began to emit the steady series of beeps that always preceded final arming of the system. "I've got thirty seconds, right? I'll hurry on out of here so it doesn't go off. Call me if you need to talk. I know you still have my number. Goodbye, Pete."

She turned away from him and walked hurriedly out of the kitchen.

SIX

Pete was still standing in the kitchen with his mouth hanging open when he heard the front door open and then swing solidly shut. The sound snapped him out of the momentary mental paralysis. He rushed out of the kitchen and through the little hallway into the living room. Seconds later, he was at the front door, lifting a blind slat to peer out the window.

Mary's Mazda convertible was parked behind his car in the short driveway. The little red car's top was down. Of course it was. It was a nice day. Mary looked even more strikingly attractive in the bright sunlight. The way it brought out the highlights in her hair triggered a faint ache of longing somewhere inside him. The feeling was tempered, however, by the shock he was feeling in the wake of the revelation that she knew his alarm code. The code he'd never shared with her or anyone else. He supposed she must have surreptitiously observed him entering the code at some point while they were dating and had committed it to memory. It was the only thing that made any sense.

His head was buzzing with the implications, which ranged from merely disquieting to outright scary. At the center of it all was the realization that her knowledge of the code provided a possible partial explanation for why he hadn't heard the alarm go off when the dead woman's body was brought into his house. Maddeningly, it also left him with many new questions, the majority of which were related to Mary's possible involvement in this mystery woman's death.

She paused to don sunglasses as she reached the convertible's driver's side door. After opening the door, she again paused and looked at the front door to Pete's house, smiling in a way that told him she knew he was watching her. Then she got in behind the wheel, closed the door, started the car, and backed out of his driveway. Once she was out in the street, her head again turned toward his house. She lifted a hand and waggled her fingers at him. After that, she tossed her head back and laughed. In the next instant, she stomped down on the gas pedal, causing the Mazda's tires to squeal for a moment on the pavement before the car shot off down the narrow residential street at high speed.

As soon as she had disappeared from sight, Pete locked the door and started pacing around the living room, repeatedly running his hands through his hair. He was unsettled by every aspect of what had just happened. There was a telling deliberateness in the things she had done. She had wanted him to see that she knew his alarm code. That was the only reason she'd entered it in front of him, not out of any fear that he would forget to do it himself. The same went for her demeanor after leaving the house, those not-so-subtle moments of mockery.

She was involved.

Maybe she hadn't personally murdered the woman on his couch, but she'd definitely had something to do with it. And the real reason she had come here this morning—possibly for the second time this same morning—had been to play with him. To make him uncomfortable and see how he was handling the situation with the corpse. That was what all that smirking had really been about. All along she'd known the woman was dead and it had amused her to watch him desperately scramble to cover and explain.

Even in Pete's agitated state of mind, he knew what he was thinking would sound crazy to anyone he tried to tell about it. And yet he sensed it was all true. There were some glaring major puzzles pieces, things he hadn't figured out yet, but he knew in his heart his ex was a participant in a bizarre scheme against him.

Her story about overhearing a troubling conversation between Shane Watson and his pal had almost certainly been a total fabrication. He didn't doubt Shane was involved. Those ugly bruise marks around the dead woman's throat had to be his handiwork. However, it now struck Pete as possible that Mary had been the instigator of this thing rather than the other way around. Perhaps it was even probable rather than just possible.

He thought about the cold and abrupt way Mary had broken things off with him all those months ago. Up until this morning, her behavior since then had been right in line with that. She hadn't seemed to care one bit about him all that time, but now he was supposed to believe she was so worried about him she just had to pay him a personal visit to warn him of an imminent threat?

Bullshit.

She had sneakily committed his alarm code to memory and hadn't forgotten it after more than half a year. This implied a disturbing level of calculation. She had wanted to know the code for some future use. The code was one thing. He could grasp how she'd acquired that knowledge. To get into his house, though, she would also need a key. His only house key was still in his possession. It was where he left it every night at bedtime, on a ring with his other keys in the top drawer of his nightstand. He'd checked to confirm this during his earlier tour of the house checking for signs of forced entry. He couldn't imagine how he ever could have unknowingly lost track of the key long enough for some ill-intentioned person to secretly have a duplicate made, but it was the only real possibility. Mary must have pulled it off somehow, and, again, it must have happened during the period when they were dating. The biggest part of it he couldn't understand was *why* she would have done any of these things. Why do them and then wait all this time to enact this next-level psychopathic plot against him?

His phone rang.

48

He stopped pacing as his gaze snapped toward the coffee table, where he'd left the phone while he'd been engaged in the process of trying to conceal the truth about the woman on his couch. A name appeared on the screen.

Mary.

He snatched up the phone, accepted the call, and put the device to his ear. "Why are you doing this to me?"

She giggled. "I wish I could see your face right now. I bet your expression is priceless."

Pete started grinding his teeth in frustration and anger.

He said nothing.

Another giggle came over the line. "Ooh, I can sense how mad you are even through the ether. So I guess you've started figuring some things out. But not everything, Pete, my dear. Not even close to everything, I'd wager."

Pete forced himself to unclench his jaw. "Why are you doing this to me?"

She heaved an exaggerated sigh. "God, you sound like a broken record. To get to the root of the mystery, you'll have to ask better questions. With luck, you may eventually come to understand why I targeted you. It's complicated. At the root of it, though, is a simple concept. Fun."

Pete frowned. "What? You decided to kill a woman and fuck with me for *fun*? Are you insane?"

She made a tsk-tsk sound. "Now, Pete, don't go making crazy accusations. I haven't killed anybody. And you should probably be careful about saying such things on a cell phone. You never know who might be listening."

Pete felt a flicker of paranoia. He dimly recalled hearing of devices one could purchase to monitor cell phone calls. He also was pretty sure they were illegal, at least for use by anyone not working with the FBI or other high-level law enforcement agencies, but that wouldn't matter much to the morally unscrupulous.

The bottom line was Mary was right. He was angry and frustrated and wanted to know exactly what was happening to him and why, but there were certain aspects of this ordeal he shouldn't be talking about on a phone. He would have to be more vague in general and definitely *not* mention the dead woman again.

He sighed. "Does this have anything at all to do with what happened to Shane yesterday or is it all some weird-ass vendetta you have against me?"

Her laughter was louder and wilder this time, more like a cackle. "Ooh, 'vendetta'. I like that. It makes me sound like some kind of crazy badass chick in a movie. Which I totally am, by the way. Except for the movie part. And, yes, Shane's a part of this. But only a little part. I'm the brains. The one in charge. I've had you in mind for this for a long time."

"I don't understand. Why are you—"

"That's all the information you get for now," she said, cutting him off. "I'm not giving the whole game away all at once, silly boy."

Pete grunted. "You know what? Maybe I'll just bite the bullet and go to the cops with this. I'm a human being, not some goddamn plaything in a lunatic's game."

"You may want to rethink that attitude, you slimy little worm of a man." Mary's tone was frostier when she resumed speaking, the playfulness displaced by a simmering rage. "Like it or not, you're already in up to your neck in this thing. There's so much you don't know yet. You think you have a choice, but you don't. If you try to get out of it, things will get worse for you. Much worse."

Pete frowned. "Worse? How could things get any worse?"

A protracted silence from the other end.

A knot of dread formed in Pete's stomach as he pondered the meaning of her statement. He had a feeling his life had just been threatened. Mary simply hadn't made the threat explicit for the same reason she'd admonished Pete for his reference to the dead woman.

Mary icily said, "I promise you this, Pete. I don't say such things idly. If I tell you not to do something or else, you better damn well not do it. Understand?"

Pete swallowed a lump in his throat and again started to slowly pace about the living room. He felt helpless and afraid. And alone. There was no one he trusted enough to reach out to for advice or assistance. He felt like he was on the verge of curling up in a fetal ball and bawling like a baby. Given his increasingly bleak state of mind, total mental collapse was a real option.

Except that it wasn't and he knew it. That was the side of his personality that had held sway for far too long in his life. The weak side. The side prone to capitulation in all things. He couldn't afford to let it dictate his actions in this matter. And he would have to be as canny and calculating as his adversaries.

"I asked you a question, Pete. I expect an answer. Do you understand what I'm telling you?"

Pete cleared his throat. "I understand."

"Good. As long as you behave and do as you're told, you might yet come out of this okay. Here's the main thing you need to keep in mind for now. The, uh … *item* we left for you in your house is not to be moved or disposed of until we say so."

Pete stopped pacing.

He took the phone away from his ear and scowled at the screen in disbelief a moment before again putting it to his ear. "Why not?"

"Because I fucking said so."

Pete grunted. "This is a frame job, isn't it? You're gonna make me sweat for a while and then tip off the cops."

"This is nothing so simple as an ordinary frame job, Pete. You have my word on that."

"Your word isn't worth shit."

A brief silence.

Then Mary said, "You should probably refrain from insulting me. Apologize."

Pete's face twisted with barely suppressed anger as he bit back a silent curse. He forced himself to calm down before responding, drawing in and letting out a big breath. "I'm sorry."

Mary laughed. "Apology accepted, but don't push me. I want only sniveling obsequiousness from you. That shouldn't be a problem. Just be yourself."

Pete didn't respond to that, just gripped the phone a little harder.

A sound he recognized as the flicking of a cigarette lighter came from the other end. "Later today, you'll receive a text with instructions regarding what to do with the item. Do nothing until then, little man."

The line went dead.

Pete tossed the phone on the coffee table and put his hands over his face. He groaned and, in a moment, took the hands away. He looked at the dead woman and said, "How in God's name do I get out of this?"

She had no answers for him.

SEVEN

Pete spent some time unsure of what to do with himself after Mary hung up on him. Not for the first time that day, he felt utterly helpless, like a man stuck in limbo. Unless a better option unexpectedly materialized, all he could do was wait around until he received the promised text, a message he knew might never come. The promise of it might be nothing more than another tactic in the campaign of psychological torture Mary was waging against him.

But he believed he would hear from her again.

It might be hours from now, though. Perhaps *many* hours.

What was he to do with himself until then?

With no immediate answers springing to mind, he wandered into the kitchen, where he paused for a moment and stared at his coffeemaker. If his Saturday morning had proceeded in the usual way, he would already be halfway through his first pot of the day. He considered putting on a pot now, but opted against it. Once he got started on the java, he could see himself going through pot after pot. Too much coffee would give him the jitters and he felt twitchy enough as things stood.

There was the opposite end of the beverage spectrum to consider, though. He went to the fridge, pulled open the door, and peered inside. Pete didn't drink alcohol much. He still had three bottles of Budweiser left over from a six-pack he'd purchased two weekends ago. Maybe the beer would calm his nerves. He hesitated, thinking about it. Three beers might do that job nicely, but it might also impede his ability to think clearly. That would be bad. There was also a single bottle of Diet Coke. He made a face. The soda wasn't an option that pleased him, but it would have to do for now.

He took the Diet Coke out of the fridge and walked back out to the living room, where he slowly twisted off the cap and stared at the feminine form hidden beneath the blanket. The prospect of spending untold hours with only a brutally murdered corpse for company was not an enticing one.

Pete took a big swig from the soda bottle and winced. He'd forgotten how much he disliked diet soft drinks. Come to think of it, he couldn't remember having bought a Diet Coke any time recently. Now he looked at the bottle and tried to remember having seen it there in the past. Perhaps it'd been a random, forgotten purchase from weeks or months ago, something he'd snagged from a convenience store after stopping to put gas in his car after work. No. There was nothing like that—not even the vaguest hint of it—in the foggiest corners of his memory. Not only that, but he was certain the soda bottle hadn't been in his fridge last night. Now he was thinking about opening the bottle. His heart started hammering faster as he realized he couldn't remember hearing the sound of the seal breaking when he twisted the cap.

"Oh, shit."

Pete ran into the kitchen and dumped the bottle in the sink. He then bent over and shoved a finger down his throat, probing hard until he made himself gag. A liquid mix of bile and something dark that might have been traces of the soda dripped into the sink. Realizing that most of the soda would not be coming back up made him whimper with fear. In that moment, he was convinced the soda had been left in his fridge as an insidious trick on the part of his tormenters. It was laced with poison or some strange psychoactive drug that would cause him to hallucinate and make him feel like he was going crazy. He stood shaking above the sink for several minutes, his hands braced on the edge of the counter as he waited to either die or start freaking out.

Neither of those things happened.

He did, however, begin to feel drowsy. His eyes felt bleary and his eyelids began to droop. A deep yawn came out of nowhere. He stepped back from the sink to rub at his eyes and yawned again. This was disconcerting. He shouldn't feel this tired, not this soon after having slept so solidly through the night. There was no denying the physical reality, though. He felt an almost overwhelming urge to go lie down and close his eyes, maybe take a long nap.

He glanced at the now-empty plastic soda bottle sitting on the counter by the sink. The soda had been laced with something, but not with poison or hallucinogens. Instead it had been dosed with some kind of powerful knockout drug. He started trying to puzzle out why Mary might have done such a thing. It didn't seem necessary. He was already caught in her trap, a prisoner in his own home, his future subject to her sadistic whims. The randomness of it also made it odd. He was convinced now the soda had been dosed. The sleepiness was intensifying seemingly by the moment, with yawn after deep, jaw-cracking yawn repeatedly prying his mouth open. He had definitely been drugged. And yet there had never been any guarantee of him drinking that soda. That he had done so was, in fact, highly unusual. So why dose the bottle and put it in his fridge?

Turning away from the counter, he stumbled over to the fridge and hauled the door open again, peering inside through eyes that had never felt so bleary. He looked at that half-empty six-pack of Budweiser, trying to remember whether it had been that close to the edge of the top shelf last night. He didn't think so. And, unlike the fancy craft beers so many of his acquaintances enjoyed, those Bud bottles had twist-off caps. Mary could have opened them, dosed them all, and then put the caps back on. He frowned as he continued to stare at the six-pack. There was something else off about it, but his increasingly foggy thinking made it difficult to pinpoint what that might be.

Then it came to him.

The brown bottles were all in slots along one side of the carton. He was sure the bottles had been arranged differently in the carton before last night, with one open slot on one side and two open slots on the other. That clinched it for him. The beer had been dosed, too. He had to assume the same was true for the carton of milk and bottle of orange juice, both of which sat inside one of the door shelves. He stepped back from the fridge, allowing the door to swing slowly shut as his gaze went to the can of Folgers next to the coffeemaker. He took a shaky step toward it and nearly fell over. His movements felt sluggish now, as if he were walking underwater at the bottom of a swimming pool.

He slapped himself in the face and tried to force his eyes to open wider. This had no discernible effect on the steadily deepening mental fogginess. He bit down on his bottom lip nearly hard enough to draw blood. Oops. Check that. There was a slight tang of saltiness in his mouth. He *had* drawn a little blood, after all. The sharp sting of pain helped a little, making him slightly more alert as he arrived at the coffeemaker and reached for the can of Folgers. He pried off the plastic top with fumbling, numb fingers, slapping it down on the countertop. His head wobbled on his shoulders and he felt close to falling over, but he garnered a few more moments of semi-awareness with another, much harder slap across the face. While the sting of this second blow was still fresh, he dipped a finger down into the coffee grains and began to swirl them around. It didn't take long to spy faint traces of a white powder mixed in with the brown grains.

The bitch had dosed *everything*. She was thorough, if nothing else. He had to give her that. His finger caught against the rim of the Folgers can as he pulled it away, causing the can to slide off the counter and fall to the floor, spilling coffee grains and white powder all over the tiles. He saw now that there'd been more of the mystery drug hidden in the grains than he'd originally suspected. He believed the drug was some kind of strong sedative rather than a poison, but it seemed possible an overdose of it might put him in a coma or even kill him. He didn't believe that was Mary's intent. She'd gone to a lot of trouble to mess with his head and put this scheme together. But she wasn't a medical professional. She could have made a mistake with the dose.

Pete knew he should feel much more alarmed by this possibility than he did, but he was feeling more detached from his emotions and the world around him with each passing second. He staggered out of the kitchen and went into the living room. His phone was still on the coffee table, where he'd left it. He picked it up with his numb fingers and cradled it in both hands to keep from dropping it. As he stood there and worked as hard as he could to stay on his feet, he tried to think who among his acquaintances might be able to speedily procure him some cocaine. It stood to reason that a heavy-duty stimulant like coke might counteract the effects of whatever Mary had used to drug him. Or would it? He didn't know for sure if it would work like that. He wasn't any more of a drug guy than he was a booze guy. He'd never snorted coke in his life. It seemed like he probably knew one or two people from work who were fiends for the stuff, but he was having trouble dredging their names up from the murky depths of his drug-fogged brain.

The phone slipped from his fingers and landed with a sharp slapping sound on the hardwood floor. A few seconds later, the remaining strength seeped out of Pete's legs, his eyes rolled back in his head, and he dropped to his knees, remaining partly upright another moment longer before pitching over onto his side. Within a few more moments, he was snoring deeply while drool dribbled from the corner of his mouth.

EIGHT

Pete's eyes remained closed as he began to drift back toward consciousness. His thoughts were still fuzzy from sleep and the drug he'd inadvertently ingested, but he dimly sensed a significant amount of time had passed. In those initial moments of gray semi-consciousness, he didn't remember much about what had happened before he passed out. There was a vague sense of things being seriously amiss in some way, but that was about it.

Mary.

The name was the first word that formed clearly in his head as he began to wake up. The only Mary he knew was Mary Wilson from work. An image of her face came into focus in his head. Her expression was a strange one, with a hint of something sly and devious. At first this only confused him. He dreamed of

Mary sometimes, which was only natural, given that she was the last woman with whom he'd been semi-intimate. He found the dreams vaguely annoying because of the cold way she had dumped him, but they had never been outright troubling.

Until now.

Pete's eyelids began to flutter and he yawned as they rose to half-mast. He still wasn't really seeing anything, just blurred colors and shapes, but he soon realized he was no longer on the floor. He was at a higher elevation now. Above the floor, but not in his bed, because what was beneath him wasn't quite as comfortable as his soft mattress. Was he on the couch in the living room?

He thought he probably was.

And hold on a minute ... why had he been passed out on the floor in the first place?

The vague sensation of dread sharply intensified. He realized he was not lying flat on the cushions of the couch itself. There was a lumpen something else beneath him. Something that felt like the flesh of another human being. Only there was something off about it. Physical sensation sharpened. There was definitely another body beneath his own. He sensed it was a woman. And he was lying naked between her splayed legs.

Pete's eyes snapped all the way open and he stared directly into the unseeing eyes of the dead woman. He screamed. Then it all came back to him in an instant. The discovery of the corpse in his living room. The visit from Mary. Her threats. Drinking the drugged soft drink and passing out on the floor.

He trembled as he began to see in his head what must have happened. Mary had returned to the house while he was unconscious, letting herself in with the duplicate key she'd mysteriously acquired. Shane Watson had probably been with her this time. He couldn't see her doing the heavy physical work of undressing his unconscious form, lifting it off the floor, and arranging it in this hideous parody of a carnal coupling. Not because she couldn't, but because she wouldn't have *wanted* to do it. And why bother when she had a musclebound lackey in tow to do her bidding?

He had been set up to look like he was having sex with a corpse, but to what purpose? Was it just another way of messing with his head? That was almost certainly a part of it, but he thought there was more to it than that. He pictured Mary standing over him with her phone aimed at the couch, smirking as she took a series of compromising photos. Photos that made him look like the worst kind of sick bastard. Like a necrophiliac. The instant the possibility occurred to him, he became certain it had happened. There was no reason she *wouldn't* have done it, given the circumstances. And that meant she now had in her possession blackmail material that could ruin him if he failed to do anything other than precisely what she told him to do from here on out.

Pete groaned.

I am so fucked.

He pushed himself up and glanced at the blind covering the large window above the couch. Only blackness was visible through the small gaps between the slats. It was night now. As he'd sensed, a lot of time had passed. His gaze returned to the body of the woman beneath him, who was lovely even in death. The body was entirely nude now, the lacy black bra and panties having been removed. A part of him wanted nothing more than to get off the couch and away from her, but he became briefly entranced by the sight of her bare breasts. They were a nice size and shape, exquisitely rounded, the nipples large and pink. His gaze drifted down to her flat belly and then moved even farther down, toward her shaved vagina. He stared at her exposed genitals a moment before beginning to feel uncomfortable, more like a real pervert rather than just a poor schmuck who'd been drugged and duped into looking like one. It made him feel dirty and inhuman. Like the worst kind of creep. It was a feeling he hated.

Even so, a slimy impulse rose up from the darkest, foulest depths of the most primitive part of his brain, what head doctors called the lizard brain. An impulse to reach out and cup those beautiful breasts in his hands. He swallowed hard as he envisioned himself doing it. The way the breasts would feel against the soft flesh of his palms was something he sensed so palpably it felt close to tactile reality. He could almost feel the spongy resistance of her nipples as he pressed the balls of his thumbs against them. He let out a breath and felt a touch of heat in his cheeks. His cock twitched and began to swell.

What the fuck is wrong with me?

Pete abruptly got up off the couch and staggered backward

into the center of the living room, horror at the awful thing he'd been contemplating rising up inside him like a rapidly spreading sickness. He was filled with disgust and self-loathing. But there was also anger. This wasn't the real Pete Adler. He wasn't a scumbag. Never in his life had he entertained such repulsive thoughts. Not until today. This was a product of stress and ma- nipulation. He was a victim, too, just like this woman. Well, not *just* like her. She was dead, after all, and he was still alive, at least for the time being. In a way, though, she was lucky. For her, this was over. He was *still* being victimized, with no end to his ordeal in sight.

He decided the first thing he should do was cover the naked corpse. That should at least help dull the sick necro-erotic im- pulse still whispering to him from the back of his tortured brain. The blanket he'd covered her with earlier in the day had been swept to the floor. He was about to kneel and reach for it when he belatedly took note of something else at the edge of his pe- ripheral vision.

No. Please, no.

He let out a breath and turned slowly toward the recliner. What he saw there elicited a high-pitched shriek, followed by a quieter whimper of helplessness. He felt like crying. Seated in the recliner was the body of a second dead woman. As with the corpse on the couch, a lot of bare flesh was exposed. In this woman's case, however, her private areas were still covered by lacy underwear garments. A red pentagram adorned the crotch of her black panties. She was also wearing a pair of stiletto platform heels similar to the shoes worn by the first woman. Some tattoos were visible, but she wasn't quite as profusely inked as the woman on the couch. Her big mane of hair was a shade of blonde that clearly came from a bottle. An open handbag sat on the floor next to the recliner. Clues to her identity were probably inside it.

Pete had resisted investigating the contents of the first woman's purse out of fear of smearing his DNA all over her belongings, but his body had been mashed against the corpse of the black-haired woman for an unknown period of hours. Traces of him were all over her corpse. Contaminating the second woman's belongings with his DNA seemed inconsequential now. He decided he would dig through both bags and find out as much as he could about these unfortunate women. Knowing their names might not benefit him in any meaningful way, but some information would be better than nothing. At the very least, it would allow him to stop thinking of them as "Dead Woman No. 1" and "Dead Woman No. 2".

First, though, there was something else he had to do.

Pete went into his bedroom to put on some clothes.

NINE

A check of the alarm panel in the kitchen showed that Mary had not bothered resetting the system after leaving this latest time. This didn't surprise Pete. She had reset the alarm the first time only as a means of confounding him. It had been a crucial element in the first part of this thing she was doing. This campaign of psychological torment.

After getting dressed, Pete had second thoughts about rooting through the handbags that had apparently belonged to the dead women. This was symptomatic of a larger overall pattern of indecisiveness. He was plagued by doubts about how to proceed at every turn. And every moment he spent alone in the house in the presence of the murdered women exacerbated the anxiety he was feeling. He started to feel suffocated in his own home and was soon consumed with a need to get out, at least for a short while.

He considered arming the alarm system again before leaving, but opted against it, deciding he didn't give a damn if some hapless burglar came into the house and discovered the bodies in his living room. He still had no interest in voluntarily involving the authorities in this gruesome business, but if some other person informed on him, so be it.

He closed the front door as he left the house, but didn't lock it. He stared at the door a moment before stepping down from the porch, thinking maybe he should reconsider. Not setting the alarm was one thing. Failing to secure the front door felt like a bigger step down the slippery slope of tempting fate.

Fuck it.

Pete turned away from the door and descended the steps to the sidewalk. After getting behind the wheel of his car and starting the engine, he took a moment to check his phone before backing out of the driveway. Mary had promised he'd get a text with instructions about what to do next, but there was nothing when he swiped the screen to bring it to life. No voicemails. Not a single text. Weird. Maybe she just hadn't gotten around to sending the promised message yet. Or maybe she'd never actually-ly meant to send a text at all. Telling him to expect one and then not following through might well have been nothing more than another way of fucking with his head.

Pete sighed and tossed the phone on the empty passenger seat.

Whatever.

He backed out of the driveway, changed gears, and began to drive out of his neighborhood. Within a few minutes, he was sitting at the intersection of Maplewood and Thorpe. A turn to the right and a drive of just a few more blocks would take him to the nearest convenience store. When it became his turn to move through the four-way stop, he cranked the wheel to the right and hit the gas. In another few moments, he pulled into the store's parking lot and parked in a space right out front.

Pete had decided inebriation was the only way he could deal with the colossally fucked-up situation facing him. Under the circumstances, he couldn't conceive of a more effective means of calming his jangling nerves. His usual commitment to moderation wasn't something he would choose to abandon lightly. Too many of his relatives had been terrible alcoholics, which was why he'd always exercised such rigid self-control when it came to booze. He didn't care about that right now, though. Tonight he would unleash that familial demon along with all its terrible potential.

Before he could get out of the car, his phone rang. He glanced at the passenger seat, where the phone still rested, and saw Mary's number on the screen. Scowling, Pete got out of the car, throwing the door shut without locking it as he strode rapidly toward the glass doors at the front of the store. Yes, he would have to talk to the bitch again, probably very soon, but this one time at least he wouldn't be her dancing monkey.

He banged through the doors in an aggressive way that wasn't like his normal self at all, nearly knocking over a young black man with dreads in the process. Dreads Guy was on his way out of the store. He came close to dropping the paper sack in his hands as Pete pushed past him and kept moving at a fast pace toward the back of the store. The guy yelled something at Pete about how he should watch where he was going. For a second or two there, Pete feared he'd made a fatal miscalculation in his state of blind agitation.

He didn't like to think of himself as racist, but he couldn't help making a kneejerk correlation between this guy and pictures of young thugs he often saw in local crime news reports. His imagination, already in a state of feverish overdrive, supplied him with an image of Dreads Guy pulling a Glock out of his baggy pants and coming after him. A backward glance, however, showed that the young man had already left the store. Pete relaxed but felt a twinge of guilt for his thoughts.

His attention returned to the beer cooler in front of him. It was the wrong one. This one was full of a bunch of craft beers hipsters and many of his coworkers enjoyed. Maybe some of them were good. Pete had no real clue in that department. Because he drank so little normally, he'd always been a man of simple tastes when it came to beer.

He sidled over one door and saw cartons of Bud, Miller Lite, Pabst, and the like. This was the right door. It was stocked with what the beer snobs called "piss water". He opened it and reached for a six-pack of Bud, but he hesitated when he saw the twelve-pack cartons on the lower shelves. He'd never purchased anything above a six-pack. Ordinarily he never had a need to have a higher quantity of beer on hand than that. But things had changed and he had a feeling a mere six beers wouldn't cut it tonight.

The clerk gave him his total. He extracted some bills from his wallet and slapped them on the counter. After the clerk handed over his change, Pete grabbed his twelve-pack and got the hell out of the store. Outside on the sidewalk, he saw Dreads Guy again. He was leaning against the wall and smoking a cigarette. Pete couldn't help audibly gasping.

The guy gave him a curious look and said, "The fuck is your problem?"

On closer look, this wasn't the same guy at all. It was just another young black man with dreadlocks. Pete smiled nervously and shrugged a wordless apology. He felt terrible for his knee-jerk racial profiling, but at least he had a decent excuse. He wasn't his normal self. No, not all. He felt on edge and perpetually on the verge of screaming.

Back in his car, Pete started the engine and reached for the gearshift. Before he could back out of the parking space, his phone rang again. He glanced at it and saw Mary's name and number on the screen. His hand stayed on the gearshift a moment as he considered again ignoring her call. The spark of defiance that had propelled him out of the car began to fade as he realized she'd probably also tried calling while he was in the store. Repeatedly calling in such a short time frame implied a possibly dangerous level of irritation on Mary's part.

He sighed. "Fuck."

Grabbing the phone, he hit the answer button, and put the device to his ear. "What?"

"What a rude way to answer the phone. Where have your manners gone, Pete?"

He grunted. "Down the fucking drain, right along with the lives of the dead strippers in my house."

A brief silence ensued. Then came a chuckle. "You're a funny guy, Pete. Dead strippers. Such a morbid sense of humor."

Pete reached over to the footwell in front of the passenger seat, where he'd set the beer carton. He ripped the carton open, fished out a can of Bud, and popped it open as he sat up straight behind the wheel again. The can was slippery with condensation and he had to grip it tight in his left hand to maintain his hold on it.

"Hmm. That sounded suspiciously like someone opening a beer."

Pete took a big swig of cold Budweiser. "That's because I just opened a beer. Congratulations. You're a fucking genius."

Dreads Guy number two had moved down the sidewalk and now stood directly in front of Pete's car. He made no threatening moves, but he gave Pete the evil eye as he took another drag on his cigarette.

"Don't get snotty with me, Pete. It isn't a good idea and doesn't suit you, anyway."

Pete slugged back more beer and laughed. "What would you know about what suits me? Hell, what would you know about anything other than being a psychotic fucking bitch?"

Silence from the other end.

Pete met the gaze of the man eyeing him from the sidewalk and raised his can in what he hoped came across as a friendly salute.

Dreads Guy number two just sneered and shook his head.

The silence from the other end dragged on at least a full minute. Pete chugged down the entire contents of his first beer before Mary resumed speaking. He crushed the empty can and tossed it to the floor.

Mary sighed. "So … feeling like a tough guy all of a sudden, eh? I've cautioned you against addressing me in a disrespectful manner and assumed you'd gotten the message, but it seems your attitude could use some further adjusting."

Pete leaned over and dragged a second can of Bud out of the torn-open carton. He sat up straight again and popped open the tab, tensing for a moment when he saw a police cruiser pull into the parking space next to him. In that instant, he was convinced he was on the verge of being arrested. The police had discovered the corpses in his house and had somehow tracked him down in record speed. But that didn't happen. Instead, the cop got out of his cruiser and stepped up to the sidewalk. Dreads Guy number two flicked his cigarette butt onto the hood of Pete's car and approached the cop, engaging him in conversation.

Uh-oh.

Pete interpreted this development as his cue to finally leave. Setting the second Bud can in a cupholder, he kept the phone to his ear as he backed out of the parking space, got his car turned around and pointed back toward the street. He hit the gas and took off. "My attitude is just fine. In fact, I'd call it appropriate to the fucking circumstances. You know what? Knock yourself out. Do your fucking worst. I don't even care anymore."

Mary snorted derisively. "Your phony bravado doesn't fool me, Pete. You're feeling brave right now, but that won't last. Sooner or later, you'll start thinking in a more rational way again and be right back to your usual sniveling, pitiful self. Meanwhile, here's some food for thought. Did you ever consider that leaving your house tonight of all nights might not have been the wisest idea?"

A chill went through Pete as he neared the intersection of Maplewood and Thorpe. Mary's assessment proved accurate as he felt some of his bluster begin to leach away. "What are you talking about?"

He winced as he heard a shameful hint of whining creep back into his voice.

Mary laughed. "Oh, Pete. You poor idiot. Did you think I wouldn't have someone keeping an eye on your house?"

Pete had trouble breathing for a moment as the fear rose up inside him again. He swallowed with difficulty and cleared his throat. "I don't believe you. You wouldn't keep Shane or anyone else lurking around outside all this time. A neighbor would notice eventually and call the cops to report suspicious activity."

"Which is why he isn't lurking around outside."

Mary laughed again.

She knew he'd left the house. That much was indisputable. So maybe she did have someone keeping an eye on his place. Pete's pulse quickened as an alarming alternate possibility came to him. He hadn't conducted another thorough search of the house prior to his departure, which meant it was technically possible Shane or some other lackey had still been inside it. A belated shiver of dread coursed through him at the thought.

"Shane's in my house, isn't he?"

Mary chuckled. "He's in a house. Not necessarily yours, though."

Pete frowned. "What's that supposed to mean?"

"Now, Pete, you should know by now I have no interest in spelling everything out for you. I'll just say this. You have some surprises in store once you get home, including possibly a clue or two. You're not entirely stupid, despite frequent appearances to the contrary. You'll be able to figure out some things. Goodbye, Pete. We'll talk again soon."

She disconnected the call.

TEN

Pete forced himself to slow down as he turned down his street, pumping the brake pedal and relaxing his grip on the steering wheel. He didn't want to draw unwanted attention by roaring down the street and coming to a squealing stop in his driveway. His breathing evened out and his heart rate began to slow as he guided his car slowly down the street. Going out for the beer had been a mistake. This was a thing that should have been obvious from the outset, of course. He'd allowed the stress of the situation to get the better of him, something he couldn't let happen again.

This brief period of relative calm ended the moment his house came into view. His breath caught in his throat and his hands clenched around the steering wheel when he saw what was on his porch.

He shook his head and whimpered. "Oh, my fucking god."

Dead woman number two had been put out on his porch. The busty blonde-haired corpse was sitting in a slumped position with her back against the closed screen door, her arms hanging limp at her sides. Gripped loosely in her left hand was one of the tainted Budweiser bottles from his fridge. The porch light he'd left off when leaving had been turned on, making the corpse's presence there difficult to miss for anyone who might happen by.

He goosed the gas pedal to close the remaining distance to his house a bit more quickly, turning into the driveway and shutting off the engine immediately. Getting the dead woman back into his house and out of sight was his top priority, of course, but instead of getting out of his car right away, he twisted around in his seat, craning his head this way and that in search of any nosy neighbors who might be in the area. Not seeing anybody, he got out of the car, eased the door quietly shut, and jogged up to the porch, where he stopped and turned around for another quick scan of the street. Still nobody in sight.

Maybe he'd gotten lucky here and no one had yet spotted the corpse on his porch. He thought it was possible. He hadn't been gone long, after all, and the scene on his porch had been staged in a way that made it look as if the woman had simply passed out after drinking too much. Someone might have come over to check on her if she'd been left out here for an extended period, but that appeared not to have happened yet. He wasn't out of the woods yet, though. He needed to work fast to keep things that way.

The body slid slowly sideways as Pete eased the screen door open and unlocked the front door. Taking out his key and inserting it in the lock was pure muscle reflex. He did it because he always did it when coming home. Only after turning the key in the lock, however, did he remember that he'd left it unlocked when he'd gone out. The click he heard when turning the key suggested that had not remained the case for the duration of his absence. Shane must have locked the door after dragging the dead woman outside. It seemed an odd thing for him to have done under the circumstances. Then again, everything about the situation was odd.

To understate.

He glanced around again as he pushed the door open a few inches and was again relieved to find he still wasn't being observed, at least not by anyone he could see. Reaching through the opening, he patted his hand along the wall until he found the light switches. He flipped one down and the porch light went out. The disappearance of the light afforded him a short-lived moment of relief. The dead woman would be harder to see now for anyone who might drive by, but any sense of being out of danger was illusory. A police cruiser on routine patrol might happen by at any moment. Shane was probably still lurking around somewhere out here. The extinguishing of the porch light made the deeper darkness outside his house feel creepier. He imagined Shane moving stealthily through the shadows with a knife in his hand, inching closer and closer and getting ready to pounce.

Pete grabbed the dead woman under her arms, opened the screen door again with the toe of his shoe, and grunted in exertion several times as he dragged the body inside. A sheen of sweat had formed on his forehead by the time he dumped the corpse in the middle of the living room floor. He stood there panting for a moment, his heart racing. The woman couldn't have weighed much more than 120 pounds or so, judging from her height and build, but Pete was a slightly built man unaccustomed to hauling around 120-pound loads of dead weight. Maneuvering dead woman number one into her faux-sleeping position on the couch had been hard enough, but this had been much worse.

At least it was done now. He could relax a little and allow himself a few moments to think about what to do next. He was still very much at Mary's mercy here and seemingly trapped, but that didn't mean he should quit trying to brainstorm a solution. Inspiration might strike at any moment. He needed to be ready to act when—or if—it happened.

He went to the front door with the intention of closing it, but his hand froze on the doorknob as he remembered his twelve-pack of beer. It was still in the footwell of the front passenger seat. Leaving it there and resisting the temptation that had driven him out of the house in the first place was the obvious smart thing to do. He'd already accepted that his previous impulse to get shitfaced had been misguided, but maybe just another beer or two to calm his nerves a bit more would be okay.

He eased the door open and flipped the porch light on again.

Now that the body was out of sight, having the light off wasn't necessary. Besides, on the off-chance anyone was lurking around out there, having the light on might allow him to slip out of harm's way faster.

He stepped out onto the porch and took a look around. There was still no one in the area. Deciding he didn't want to be out here any longer than necessary, Pete stepped down from the porch and jogged back over to the passenger side of his car, hitting the unlock button on his key fob twice to unlock the door. The twelve-pack was where he'd left it, in the footwell. The second can he'd taken from the carton was still in the cupholder between seats. He grabbed the carton from the floor and retrieved the open can from the cupholder. After backing out of the car and bumping the door shut with his hip, he put the lukewarm open can to his lips. Before drinking from it, however, he thought about the tainted beverages in his refrigerator. It seemed unlikely in the extreme that Shane or Mary had opened his car during the brief time he was in the house, but there was no point in taking chances. He shouldn't drink any open beverages he'd left unattended for even for the shortest amount of time.

Pete poured the rest of the beer from the open can out on his lawn and went inside, closing and locking the door behind him. He was on his way to the kitchen to stow the beer carton in the fridge when something in his peripheral vision made him stop in his tracks. There was something on the coffee table he was sure hadn't been there moments ago. Another helpless whimper escaped his lips as he turned slowly toward the coffee table.

He frowned.

What the fuck?

In the center of the coffee table rested a large, square-shaped black box. Actually, he realized upon closer inspection, the dominant color was a dark gray, with a single wide vertical black stripe running up the center of each side of the box. A velvety black bow was pinned to the top of the box. It looked like a gift box, albeit one intended for people of the goth persuasion, a description that in no way fit Pete. The presence of the box in and of itself was disturbing. He had no doubt that whatever was inside it would be even more so. The more immediate source of concern was the obvious implication that someone had come into the house and put the box on the table while he'd been out fetching the beer from his car. He'd been gone no more than a minute. The person who'd done this was either still in the house or lurking around in his back yard.

A tingling sensation at the back of his neck set Pete's teeth to jittering. He imagined someone creeping up on him from behind or watching him from just inside the second bedroom, the door to which was directly to his rear. He whirled around with a panicked gasp, raising the beer carton in preparation of smashing it against the head of an adversary.

There was no one there, though, unless you counted the dead blonde woman on the floor at his feet. Keeping the beer carton raised, he stepped over the corpse and moved lightly across the floor to the open door. His heart started beating faster as he neared that dark rectangle and the shadows beyond. No part of him wanted to do this or get even one inch closer to potential danger, but he made himself keep going. The one beer he'd had was giving him just enough courage to do this without collapsing into a puddle of trembling uselessness. Once he was at the door, he carefully reached around the door frame and felt the wall for the light switch, praying someone wouldn't grab his wrist in the dark. He didn't know what he'd do if that happened. A braver person would probably fight for all he was worth. Pete feared he would only scream and beg for mercy.

But no one grabbed his wrist.

After flipping the switch, he poked his head into the room and saw that it was empty, save for the small twin-bed no one ever slept on. Venturing into the room in a slightly less trepidatious way, he peeked under the bed and checked the closet to completely confirm the lack of a nefarious presence. He moved out of the room and pulled the door firmly shut, as if by doing this he could seal off at least that one part of the house from the evil that had invaded his life.

Deciding to stow the beer carton in his fridge and procure a better weapon, he went into the kitchen and again stopped cold in his tracks. The door to his big back yard was standing open. Through the screen door's window, he saw grass in dire need of mowing. He would normally not be able to see the grass at this hour without flipping on the back stoop light, but something had moved around back there, activating the motion sensor.

As he approached the door, he held the beer carton cradled

against his chest, instinctively putting it between himself and any danger lurking outside as a kind of makeshift shield. An utterly useless shield that would provide no meaningful level of protection against a deranged individual with a penchant for strangling scantily clad young women with his bare hands. Upon realizing the absurdity of the gesture, he decided to stow the beer carton in the fridge before checking the back yard for signs of the intruder. There was a wood knife block on the countertop next to the fridge. The big handles of the larger carving knives jutted from the slots at the top of the block. One of those would work far better as a means of defending himself. He'd grab one just as soon as he'd put the beer away.

Pete hauled the refrigerator door open and leaned in to stow the carton on the top shelf, stopping when he saw the transparent Tupperware container. It was in roughly the same place where he'd meant to put the beer carton. He tilted his head and frowned as he tried to make out what was inside the container, which had not been there earlier. It was one of the smaller containers of its type, a size meant for storing the leftover portion of an individual person's meal. The thing inside it looked like a lump of raw, bloody meat. Even without knowing precisely what it was yet, Pete began to feel queasy. There was no doubt this was yet another "gift" from his tormentors. His instinct at this point was to hurriedly put the beer away on a lower shelf and shut the door without taking a closer look at the thing in the Tupperware container.

But he knew he couldn't do that.

Turning away from unpleasant things or pretending they didn't exist was not an option at this point. Choking back the bile rising into his throat, Pete slid the beer carton onto the narrow middle shelf, grabbed the Tupperware container, and took a few steps back from the fridge. A lump formed in his throat as he held the container in his trembling hands and stared at the lid. He was whimpering again as he began to peel back a corner of the lid. The trembling in his hands intensified as the lid came off and fell to the floor. He gasped and slapped a hand over his mouth when he finally understood what he was seeing—a man's severed penis and balls.

He shrieked in startled terror when someone knocked stridently against the screen door. His head snapped in that direction and he came close to peeing his pants when he saw Shane Watson leering in at him. The big grin splitting the middle of his face had a maniacal aspect to it, an impression heightened by the blood smeared all over his cheeks and forehead. The way Pete's heart was slamming in his chest made him fear an imminent heart attack. He felt paralyzed and had no idea what he'd do if Shane opened the unlocked screen door and came into the house. A grab for one of those big knives was the obvious move, but in that moment he felt incapable of action. Shane laughed and waggled his eyebrows in a way that suggested he sensed Pete's shameful impotence. He opened his mouth wider and licked the window, leaving a slimy trail along the glass. Then he retreated from the porch and disappeared from sight.

As soon as Shane was gone, Pete rushed over to the doorway

and slammed the inner door shut. He turned the bottom lock and used his key to engage the deadbolt above it. Having this extra barrier between himself and the madman still lurking somewhere in his back yard made him feel slightly better for a few seconds. Then he realized that Shane likely was in possession of a duplicate key and the terror surged inside him again. The man could reenter the house at any time and Pete would be powerless to stop him.

He took another look at the lump of bloody flesh in the Tupperware container, experiencing another moment of intense nausea before setting the container on the stove. Feeling closer than ever to a complete mental collapse, Pete revisited the previously dismissed idea of involving the police. There was an exponentially greater level of incriminating shit present in his house now. Multiple bodies and at least one piece of another body, the bloody genitalia of a recently castrated male. That gift box and whatever horror was inside it. And that was just the stuff he knew about.

His tormentors had probably stashed away more grisly mementos in other places. He imagined opening a random drawer in the kitchen or in his bedroom and finding other bloody organs. This felt not just possible, but likely. If he summoned the cops here, he would be going to jail for sure. And trying to make anyone understand what had really happened here wouldn't be easy. It would sound like delusional craziness. He could easily see himself taking the rap for all of this and going to jail for the rest of his life. He might even get the death penalty. And yet, even with that direst of prospects on the table, calling the cops might still be his best option. The people he was dealing with tonight weren't just ruthless and vindictive. They were genuinely unhinged. *Crazy.* Even the worst of all possible legal consequences might be preferable to facing whatever insanity they still had in store for him.

He nonetheless could not quite bring himself to make the call. Not just yet. Maybe he could work himself up to it given just a few more minutes of trying to think things through. He laughed in a dry, humorless way at the thought, knowing it was willful delusion, a lie he was telling himself. The terrible truth was he was too much of a hopeless pussy to make any kind of decision one way or the other. He wasn't going to do anything other than hang around and wait for whatever horrible outcome fate had in store for him.

Pete opened the fridge and grabbed a beer from the carton. He opened the can and chugged down its contents in what was for him record time. He tossed the empty can in the sink and grabbed another one from the carton. This one he drank a touch more slowly as he carried it out to the living room and again surveyed the insane tableau in there.

Though he had no concrete verifying information, he thought it likely the dead women had been exotic dancers. Or strippers, as they were more commonly called. Mary had referred to dead woman number one as such, a description he'd unthinkingly repeated multiple times during his most recent conversation with her. It was hard not to infer knowledge of the deceased woman's occupation from a remark that had at first seemed nothing more than an educated guess, but clearly had been so much more than that.

Also, they just had that stripper look. The tiny, skimpy underthings. The big platform heels. The probable boob enhancements. The women being strippers also made sense in terms of how they'd fallen victim to the people currently making his life a living hell. Shane had either lured the women to a secondary location away from whatever sin den had employed them or he had snatched them from a club's parking lot. This wouldn't have been an easy thing to do, at least not for most people, but women liked Shane. They found him charming for some reason that would always be a mystery to Pete. He'd found a way, that was all there was to it.

As far as Pete was concerned, the bigger mystery was the severed penis and balls currently sitting in a plastic container on his stove. He thought about it as he sipped beer and stared at the gift box on the coffee table. A third person had been murdered. A man this time. He had a hunch a bigger clue regarding that part of it lurked inside the goth-y gift box.

He knew he was meant to open the box and take a look inside, but he was reluctant to do so in the aftermath of what he'd found waiting for him in his refrigerator. The beer can felt loose and slippery in his hand, which was shaking again. He tightened his grip on it and brought the can to his mouth, tilting his head back and chugging down the rest of its contents. When it was empty, he tossed the can aside and it skittered across the hardwood floor until hitting a baseboard. He would normally never do such a thing, but keeping his house immaculately clean no longer seemed like a necessity, what with all the corpses and body parts lying around.

Pete stepped closer to the coffee table, pried the velvety top off the gift box, and peered inside, making another grisly discovery. He experienced a twinge of shock when he saw what it was, but this time the feeling was strangely muted, perhaps because by now he was expecting to encounter horrendous things at virtually every turn.

A man's severed head was inside the box's plush red interior. Biting back his revulsion, he took hold of a handful of blood-flecked hair at the top of the head and pulled it out of the box. He turned the head so he could examine its features, seeing right away that the severed extremity had belonged to someone he'd known. This was the head of Stan Richardson, his neighbor from across the street. Protruding from Stan's mouth was a folded piece of paper. Pete removed it and returned the head to the box.

He unfolded the sheet of paper and read the single sentence printed in block letters—CALL ME AS SOON AS YOU SEE THIS.

The note was unsigned, but it could only be from one person.

Pete took out his phone and made the call.

ELEVEN

Mary answered on the first ring.

"Hi, Pete? Do you like your gifts?"

Her tone was an annoyingly chirpy one. Bright and cheery in a way that was grotesque under the circumstances.

"Not especially," Pete said, scowling. "Not one damn bit, actually, but you already know that, of course."

"Gosh. You sound pretty hacked off about it."

A silent moment passed.

Then Mary giggled. "Hacked off. You get it?"

Pete groaned and rolled his eyes. "Yeah, I get it. Murder humor. How very macabre of you. Tell me something, Mary. At this point, what's to stop me from calling the cops and putting an end to this bullshit?"

Mary sighed. "Who are you kidding, Pete? You didn't do it

the last time you made that threat and you won't do it this time either. And even if you did work up the nerve to bring in the police, it'd be an even bigger mistake than you're imagining right now."

Pete frowned. "Oh, really. And why is that?"

"Because I would have no choice but to show them the dozens of graphic and upsetting photos of you being intimate with the first lovely lady who showed up at your house this morning. You must know the ones I mean, Pete. You sent them to me from your phone."

"What the fuck are you talking about?"

Mary's only answer this time was hearty laughter.

His heart beating faster now, Pete took the phone away from his ear and turned on the speaker function so he could still talk to Mary. He tapped the "photos" icon on his screen and started scrolling through pictures. Not being a big social media person, Pete rarely used his phone's camera. Unlike most people he knew, he wasn't constantly posting pictures of his food on Facebook or Instagram. Before tonight there had been less than ten photos on his camera roll. Now there were nearly forty, the vast majority of which showed him apparently fornicating with a corpse.

That the other person in the photos was deceased was made evident by some direct shots of her slack features and mangled neck. These were all posed pictures, of course. He'd been unconscious the entire time. But Mary and her murderous accomplice had done a good job arranging the bodies and framing the photos in ways that made him appear conscious and willfully engaged in the reprehensible act of necrophilia. He'd suspected she'd taken photos, but not that she'd used his phone to do it. This was bad. Really, really bad. If the police ever saw these photos, he wouldn't just get arrested on multiple counts of murder. There would be charges of corpse defilement and who knew what else.

The lurid details would get out to the media well ahead of a trial, he was sure of it. Everybody would look at him as something even lower than just a common murderer. He would become infamous, the butt of morbid jokes and the subject of a thousand true crime articles on the internet. If he went to jail, he'd become an instant target. Some other inmate would shiv him in the showers.

Another helpless whimper came out of his mouth as he shook his head in disgust and ran a hand through his hair. "You fucking bitch."

Mary laughed. "Oh, how I love making you whine. It comes so naturally to you. Doesn't it ever make you feel pathetic?"

Pete closed the camera roll and tapped his messages icon. Seeing Mary's name at the top of the list of recent messages, he tapped the preview to open the full message thread. He groaned as he scrolled through the messages, which were mostly outgoing photos sent from his phone to Mary. These were, of course, the staged corpse-fucking photos from his camera roll. Interspersed here and there between the photos were texts meant to appear as if he'd written them. These included grossly lewd comments about the images as well as threats against Mary's life, warnings that the same thing could happen to her if she didn't do as he told her.

Pete closed the message thread. "That's really fucked up, Mary. All of it."

"Thank you. I'm pretty proud of myself."

Pete grunted. "I bet you are. Just one thing, though. Who was supposed to have been taking the photos? If the cops ever see them, that's something they'll want to know."

"I'm sure." The sound of a lighter flicking came from Pete's phone. Mary said nothing further for a moment as she sparked up a cigarette and apparently took a long drag. "Good thing I already have a scapegoat in mind if necessary."

"And who would that be?"

"Who do you think?"

Feeling weary, Pete took a seat in the recliner formerly occupied by dead woman number two, whose head was now inches away from his outstretched feet. His gaze went to her slack features for a moment before moving on to her enormous bosom. He wanted to look away, but found he couldn't. The sight of them was too compelling.

"Would you really turn on Shane?"

"Of course. I'd hate to lose a fuck toy of that caliber, but I'll do whatever I have to do."

Pete shifted in the recliner, sitting up a little straighter. "I wonder what he'd say if I told him you said that. I wonder if he'd get scared enough to go to the cops with me and confess everything."

Mary took another audible deep drag on her cigarette before laughing. "He won't believe you. You have no idea how wrapped around my finger that man is. Besides, you know how stupid he is. He'd think you were making it up." Another soft laugh. "Go ahead, Pete. Tell me I'm wrong."

Pete said nothing.

"That's what I thought. Now, Pete, much as I've enjoyed our conversation. It's time for the next step in the game. And that's all this is to me. I want you to know that. A game. A fun exercise in pushing a sad little excuse for a man to his limits and beyond. Think of it not just as a game, but as a test. A test of how much you can endure before you break. And the test only gets harder as you go along. Like now, for instance. I want you to go out to your back yard. Shane is waiting there for you. You're to let him have his way with you and then he'll tell you what to do next."

Pete's eyes opened wide in alarm. "Have his way with me? What the hell does that mean?"

Mary laughed. "What do you think it means?"

Terror of what Mary's words seemed to imply made Pete stand up again and start pacing around the room. "Fuck you. I'm not going out there. No fucking way."

"You don't have a choice. I'm going to hang up now. You have one minute to get outside. If you're not out there with Shane by then, he'll let me know, at which point I start posting these photos to the police department's Facebook page. Good-bye, Pete. Say hello to Shane for me."

She laughed again.

The line went dead.

Pete stared at his phone in silent consternation for a moment.

Then he slapped himself in the forehead. *"Fuck!"*

He went into the kitchen and stared at the closed back door. That maniac was still out there. Maybe even right outside the door again. The memory of his blood-covered face pressed against the screen door's window made Pete shiver in revulsion. His breathing quickened as he recalled Mary's threat about posting the photos. He didn't really believe she would do that. Not yet, anyway. The photos going public would be bad for him, but would put her in a difficult position as well. Believing this was one thing. Being able to count on it was quite another. Mary was obviously as unhinged as Shane in her own way. She *couldn't* be counted on to act in the most rational, self-preserving way. And there was that comment about turning on Shane to consider. She likely had countermeasures already in mind for anything that might appear to implicate her.

Meanwhile, the seconds were ticking away.

"Fuck."

This time the word was enunciated as a hushed whisper rather than an aggravated shout.

He took out his keys and grabbed the longest and sharpest of the knives from the wood block. The phone went back into his pocket. His hand shook as he inserted the key in the bottom lock and turned it. The shaking intensified as he then tried to insert the key in the deadbolt lock. It took three attempts to get it in.

He had tears in his eyes as he turned it, knowing he was possibly just seconds away from being sexually assaulted by the man who'd made his work life a living hell for six months. It would be the worst of all the humiliations he'd endured at the hands of Shane Watson, which of course was the point. With every fiber of his being, he did not want it to happen. He would threaten Shane with the knife and try to keep it from happening if he could, but he was not optimistic. Shane would probably just snatch the knife from him and either toss it away or cut him with it as punishment for daring to resist.

The door was now unlocked.

He hesitated another moment longer before opening it, sniffling and wiping snot from his nose with the back of a hand. A full minute had to have passed by now. Mary might already be starting the process of posting the first of those pictures while he stood here and whimpered like a helpless baby.

Pete sucked in a big breath and cleared his throat.

Then he opened the door and went outside.

TWELVE

Pete flipped the light switch in the last instant before he stepped out onto the back stoop. The back awning's fluorescent light flickered a moment before coming fully to life. He winced as he caught a glimpse of Shane standing six feet in front of him in the yard. The blood-smeared face twisted in a snarl.

"Turn that fucking light off, bitch."

"But—"

"Do it!"

Hearing the much larger man growl and snap at him like that made Pete even more fearful. His knees were shaking so bad as he turned around and reached back into the house to flip off the light switch, he feared his legs were close to giving out under him. Somehow, though, he managed to stay upright as he closed the screen door and turned around to face Shane again. The moon was bright tonight, so he could still see the man pretty clearly at this distance. His sneering expression shifted and became an insane grin again.

"Come down off the porch, bitch." He laughed. "And put that knife away before I take it from you and jam it up your stupid fucking ass."

Pete swallowed hard upon hearing these words, unnerved by the notion of *anything* getting jammed up his ass out here tonight. He was so rattled by the thought he wound up blurting out his next words before he could think them through carefully. "Mary said she's going to kill you and frame you for all of this."

Shane laughed.

Pete frowned. "You think that's funny? Think I'm making it up?" An admonishing voice somewhere in his mind was telling him to back away from all this, that it was a miscalculation to enter such dangerous territory. He ignored the voice, figuring he'd already come too far to stop now. "I swear what I'm saying is one-hundred percent true. You're her stooge. Her scapegoat."

Shane snorted. "Oh, I believe you, fuckface. I'm not as stupid as she thinks. What you're not understanding is it doesn't matter. I decided a while ago I'd keep playing her fucked-up game until it looked like I was about to get backed into a corner I couldn't get out of. I'll see it coming, and when it does, I'll kill her and walk away from all of it. Shit, I'm not the one who's been calling and texting you all day. I've got a shit-ton more plausible deniability than that bitch."

Pete's frown deepened. "Hold on just a goddamn minute." He

waved the knife in Shane's direction. "She's forcing you to play the game, too?"

Shane's expression turned sour. "Not that it matters, bitch-boy, but, yeah, I'm a pawn just like you. She's a master of manipulation. Bitch got me fired, too."

"How did she do that?"

"She put some questionable shit on my work computer, making it look like I'd downloaded it. And I couldn't fight it because she had some other dirt on me. Stuff way worse than the work thing. Which is why I have to keep doing what she wants." Shane smirked. "For now."

"So she's blackmailing you then?"

Shane sighed. "Yeah. Again, though, it doesn't matter. If you've got any ideas in your head about talking me into teaming up with you and turning the tables on the bitch, forget it, it's not happening."

That Shane had anticipated what he'd been leading up to came as a big surprise to Pete. His impression of the man had always been that of a dumb lummox, a good-looking former jock who got by on personality and sex appeal, but wasn't all that sharp or savvy. Apparently, however, he was smarter and better at intuiting things than Pete had imagined. Perhaps, despite what he'd said, he could still be talked into seeing reason.

Pete shook his head. "You should at least consider it. You turning on her now would take her by surprise. The next time you see her, you could—"

"Let me stop you right there," Shane said, glaring at him. "I can't do anything to her, not until I'm convinced I've got no oth-er fucking choice. Shit, you think you know what she really is? You don't, okay? She's not some run-of-the-mill crazy chick hav-ing fun playing with our heads. You have no idea how truly fucking Machiavellian she is. She's not doing any of this impul-sively. Did you know she got me hired at that place? Well, she did. But that's not all. Think of the timing. I came on board there right after she broke things off with you. It wasn't a coincidence. You know how I was constantly fucking with you? Well, she told me to do all that. She's been manipulating you in lots of sub-tle little ways most of the last year. Even when she was dating you, it was part of her game. Just last night she called that part of it 'reconnaissance'." He snorted. "*That's* the kind of broad you're dealing with. A cold and calculating evil genius cunt straight from the deepest, darkest depths of hell. She's been ma-neuvering us around on her gameboard, waiting for just the right time to bring things to a head. And that time has finally come."

Pete's jaw had dropped open in abject disbelief as he listened to this speech. He willed himself to close it and swallowed before saying, "But ... that's *crazy*."

Shane smirked. "No shit."

"But why would she go to all this trouble just to fuck with us?"

Shane shrugged. "Because it amuses her. Now come down off that porch, bitch-boy. She's got me on a short leash, too, and I've already pushed my luck by taking the time to tell you how things really are. It's time to do this thing. We've got maybe five minutes left before she calls me again. At the most. This needs to be done by then. I'm warning you, though. Drop that knife before you get anywhere close to me."

Pete started trembling again. He opened his hand and the knife fell to the concrete stoop with a clatter. Fresh tears came to his eyes and he wiped them away as he stepped down to the sidewalk and then out onto the grass. He sniffled and dropped to his knees in front of Shane. Submitting to this latest and most egregious phase of his ongoing humiliation still made him queasy, but there was no way out of it he could see.

"Uh, Pete?"

Pete glanced up, feeling slightly perplexed when he glimpsed Shane's confused expression. "Yeah?"

"You mind telling me exactly what the fuck you're doing down there?"

Pete sniffled again and wiped away more tears. "M-Mary said I was s-supposed ... supposed to let you ... *have your way with me.*"

His voice rose dramatically in pitch with those last few words and the tears began to spill hotter and faster.

From Shane, there was only silence for a moment.

Then he exploded in laughter.

The display of wild, uncontrolled hilarity went on long enough that Pete began to feel vaguely embarrassed. Shane staggered several feet away from him and put a hand to his heaving belly as he continued to bellow laughter. After at least a full minute of watching this, Pete got wearily to his feet.

The last of his tears had dried up by then. He wiped the remaining moisture from his face and said, "Mind letting me in on the joke?"

Shane laughed. "Jesus Christ, man, what did you think I was gonna do? Shove my cock down your throat?"

Pete's face flushed red, his embarrassment deepening. "Um ..."

Shane laughed one last time, the sound more subdued now. "Let me guess. She insinuated something without really spelling it out, allowing your imagination to do the rest of the work for her. It was just another mind game, dude. And you fell for it, because you're the real stooge here."

His expression hardened and he abruptly came at Pete, moving too quickly for him to get out of the way or otherwise react. The man's big fist slammed into his stomach with devastating force. Pete was knocked off his feet for a fraction of a second as the air was blasted out of his lungs. When he fell back to the ground, his throat produced a reedy sound as his bruised lungs struggled to draw in air. The pain radiating outward from the center of his body was the worst he'd ever experienced. In a lifetime of being pushed around by bullies and occasionally getting punched by them, he'd never been hit anywhere near that hard. He felt crippled. Flattened. Utterly incapable of ever getting up or moving around again.

Shane was standing over him now. From this vantage point, the white ball of the moon appeared to be hanging just above his blood-smeared visage. The juxtaposition made him look even more monstrous, like some kind of vengeful and bloodthirsty creature of the night.

"That's the real reason she sent you out here, bitch-boy. So you could experience a moment of real pain, the idea being that only then could you begin to appreciate how bad things can get for you if you don't do what she wants." He craned his head around a moment, popping tendons in his neck before sighing in a way that hinted at a deep weariness. "Also, I'm supposed to deliver a message. Your instructions for the next step in the game."

Pete's only response to this was a slightly louder wheeze. Any other time, this level of pain would have occupied the whole of his consciousness. There would have been no room for contemplation of anything else. But some primal part of him fought hard to remain alert in order to focus on what Shane was telling him. His survival beyond these next few minutes might depend on it.

Shane squinted at him, appearing to assess his level of cognizance. "Still with me? I hope so. Because I'm almost out of time. You know that first dead bitch we left for you this morning? The hot black-haired one? Mary wants you to take her to the house across the street. The house has a crawlspace. You can access it through a door in the back of a hallway closet. You're to shove the dead bitch into the crawlspace and return home. At that point, you'll need to call Mary and tell her it's done. She'll let you know what to do next."

Pete drew in another breath and this time the reedy sound issuing from his throat was less severe. He was able to swallow and find enough of his voice to croak out a few words. "Is … anyone … alive over there?"

Shane looked away from him, glancing into the deeper darkness at the back of Pete's large back yard. "No."

He didn't wait around to supply more details. Instead, he took off running into that darkness. Pete propped himself up on an elbow in time to watch the man clamber over the tall privacy fence at the back of the yard and drop into the alley beyond.

THIRTEEN

A significant level of time elapsed before the pain receded to a level where Pete could get up off the ground and stagger back into his house. He moved in a halting, hunched-over fashion, his every step triggering another flash of brain-bending agony. His face was red and covered in sweat by the time he pulled open the screen door and limped into the kitchen. The screen door swung shut behind him, but he didn't bother closing the inner door. For one thing, a closed door wouldn't provide any meaningful extra level of security at this point. The people working to make a complete ruin of his life could come and go at will, so the hell with it. Also, his every movement was an exercise in painful endurance. For the time being, the physical effort required to turn around and push the door shut fell into the category of things that weren't strictly necessary.

He remained hunched over as he made his way out of the kitchen and into the hallway. The door to his bathroom was helpfully standing open. He whimpered as he moved through the doorway and then again as he forced himself to stand straight enough to open the medicine cabinet above the toilet. A big white bottle of Tylenol sat in the middle of a crowded shelf. He pushed aside some other items, grasped the bottle with a shaking hand, and held it clutched against his chest as he staggered back out to the kitchen.

Still keeping the bottle of pills clutched against his chest, he leaned against the stove and allowed himself a few moments to catch his breath. He was still experiencing sharp little stabbing sensations with seemingly each intake of air, but they became slightly less severe as his breathing became more regular. The possibility that Shane had cracked one or more of his ribs caused him significant concern in those early minutes after taking the punch. In thinking about it, however, he felt relatively confident the blow had landed too low for that. The overwhelming pain he was experiencing was instead all about the extreme level of force used to deliver the blow.

He got the pill bottle open and set it on the stovetop. He then wincingly sidestepped over to the refrigerator, pulled the door open, and bent slightly at the waist as he reached in and snagged a can of Bud from the open carton. Next he waddled back over to the stove, popped open the cold can of beer, put it to his lips, and drank deeply from it. He heaved a breath and again leaned against the stove as his teeth began to chatter. When the shiver rippling through him subsided, he shook several pills from the Tylenol bottle and washed them down with another big swig of beer. He then leaned against the stove another few minutes as he drank the remaining beer in the can and waited for the pain to hopefully start receding. Something stronger than Tylenol would have been preferable, but he had no opioids in the house. The amount of Tylenol he'd taken was three times the recommended dose. He'd have to hope it did the job.

After maybe ten more minutes of standing around, he limped back over to the fridge and took out another beer. This time pulling the door open and bending over didn't hurt quite as much. It still hurt like hell, but some marginal progress was better than nothing. Before closing the door, he decided to take the whole carton of Bud out to the living room with him. His original purpose in buying the beer had been to ease his anxiety, but now he just hoped consuming enough of it could help dull the pain. He set the carton on the stove and belatedly closed the back door.

In carrying the carton out to the living room, he discovered his breathing had almost normalized again. The little stabbing sensations only came intermittently now. He was happy about that until he saw what had been left on the recliner's seat cushion during his time outside with Shane. Another bloody lump of flesh. Mary had come into the house—apparently through the front door—while he was in the back yard. The door had been closed and locked again, a thing Pete noted dimly as he carefully sidestepped the sprawled form of dead woman number two and approached the recliner.

Standing over the recliner now, he took a closer look at the bloody lump and determined that it was a severed tongue. Face twisting in disgust, he swept it to the floor with a quick flick of his fingers and sat down with the beer carton in his lap. Despite his pain, he couldn't hold back a bit of soft, morbid laughter. Prior to everything he'd gone through today, the notion of immediately sitting his ass down in a place where a bit of someone's mutilated flesh had been resting a moment before would have been ridiculous. He couldn't possibly have done it. His revulsion would have been too intense. But things had changed. He wasn't quite the old Pete Adler anymore. Yes, in a lot of ways, he was still the same sniveling worm Mary held in such contempt, but he was now a sniveling worm who'd dragged the corpse of a murder victim into his house and had held a man's severed head in his hands. A severed penis was sitting in a Tupperware container on his stove. A tongue left on his recliner was still a disgusting thing, but he was possibly becoming a wee bit jaded.

He popped open a beer and sipped from it as he thought about why Mary had left the tongue on the recliner. Was it meant as some kind of symbolic gesture, yet another warning of what could happen to him if he went blabbing to the cops? He thought it was possible. It seemed like the kind of thing Mary would do. Or it might have no meaning at all beyond being just another attempt on her part to freak him out.

The pain continued to recede over the next several minutes as he leaned back in the recliner and drank more beer, finishing the can he'd opened upon sitting down and immediately popping the tab on another one. After another few sips from the fresh can, he turned his head toward the couch and stared at dead woman number one, trying to visualize himself carrying the corpse to the house across the street. Getting her over there and stashed away would be a difficult proposition for lots of reasons. For one thing, he lacked Shane's upper body strength. A guy like that could cradle the body in his arms and quickly carry it to the other house without breaking a sweat, whereas Pete had barely managed to drag the blonde-haired corpse in from the porch.

Dragging the body over there was seeming like his only option. He could possibly get it done that way, but it would be risky as hell. The people across the street were all dead, apparently, but he had other neighbors, and it wasn't yet late enough that they were all in bed asleep. The likelihood of one of them taking a random peek out a window at just the wrong moment was far higher than Pete would have liked. And that wasn't even taking into account motorists who might turn down the street or people out walking around. These were some of the same concerns he'd had prior to getting dead woman number two back inside, except that the risk factor would be far greater this time. Getting an apparently passed-out drunk woman in off your porch wasn't quite the same thing as openly dragging a corpse across a neighborhood street.

He sighed and shook his head, feeling hopeless as he reached the bottom of yet another can of Bud. Instead of immediately opening another one, he got up from the recliner with a grimace and set the carton and empty can on the coffee table. His bladder was feeling the strain of all the beer and he needed to go unburden it. The pain in his gut flared up slightly as he took his first shaky steps in the direction of the bathroom, but it was far duller now. He no longer felt crippled by it. In the bathroom, he flipped up the toilet seat, unzipped his pants, and began to urinate. The stream came out fast and strong and went on far longer than usual. It was only as it began to slow and come out in dribbles that a possible solution to the question of how to transport the corpse across the street came to him.

A solution that would probably require the use of an axe.

FOURTEEN

Pete went back out to the living room and approached his front door, peeking through blind slats for a look outside. No lights were on in the house across the street. Stan Richardson had lived there with his wife and a college-aged daughter for at least as long as Pete had lived in the house opposite their own, probably far longer. He hadn't known the family well, but they'd seemed nice enough. If what Shane had told him was true—and Pete thought it probably was—Stan's wife and daughter were also dead.

Of course, the needless slaughter of an entire family was tragic and unfortunate, but for Pete the lack of anyone alive over there was also fortuitous. It meant he could trespass on the property without being stopped or challenged. And going over there would be necessary to accomplish the grisly task he'd envisioned.

Okay, so Mary wanted him to transport a corpse over to that house and stash it in the crawlspace. This was problematic for all the reasons that had been troubling him, but it had occurred to him while in the bathroom that Mary had set no additional requirements regarding *how* he was to get the job done. She had not, for instance, stipulated that the corpse must remain intact. He couldn't drag the body across the street and he couldn't carry her. Not in her current form, anyway. Hacking the body into a bunch of smaller parts and carrying them over there in black trash bags, however, might just be a viable way of going about it. He wasn't much thrilled by the idea of committing a messy act of corpse mutilation, but there weren't any other workable options he could see.

There were some problems to overcome, however, the biggest one being that he didn't have an axe or any other kind of heavy-duty tool capable of dismembering the woman's body. He believed there might be a possible way around that, though. There was a storage shed in Stan's back yard. Pete had glimpsed the roof of the little building jutting over the top of the fence there numerous times over the years. Stan had been the kind of guy who appeared to actually enjoy working on his yard on the weekends. He was frequently out there trimming hedges, mowing the grass, putting down new mulch, and so forth. Pete, on the other hand, took the lazy man's way out and paid a landscaping company to come by every two weeks and do those things for him. Stan likely would never have dreamed of doing such a thing. He was a hands-on kind of guy all the way. Or had been, at least, until Shane killed him. All of which meant Stan had probably owned the full range of yard work tools.

Including, almost certainly, an axe.

Pete's path forward from here became obvious. He had to go over there, slip into the back yard, and rummage through that storage shed until he found what he wanted. He just hoped the shed wasn't locked. The house wasn't, according to Shane, but the shed might be. An image of a closed padlock hanging from a hasp came into his head, taunting him. Grimacing, he pushed the image away. He'd just have to hope for the best. If the shed *was* locked, he'd have to break into it somehow. No way around it.

Instead of opening the door and immediately heading across the street, Pete grabbed another beer from the carton, popped it open, and chugged it down as fast as he could manage. He'd consumed enough beer at this point that he'd already achieved what was, for him, a hitherto unknown level of inebriation. For most people, this was what they would call "buzzed", he supposed. That midpoint between sobriety and actual drunkenness. Pete was beginning to understand the appeal. He felt less on edge now and capable of doing things he'd normally never even consider. Maybe his father and uncles had been on to something with this drinking thing all along. Sure, they were belligerent assholes and he hoped to never see any of them again, but maybe they would have been belligerent assholes even without the booze. Who could say?

After finishing the beer, Pete opened the door and stepped

out onto his porch, easing the door shut behind him. He stepped down from the porch and walked briskly across his yard to the street, trying to move fast without running. He figured being spotted running would look more suspicious on the off-chance a neighbor did happen to look out a window and see him. He picked up his pace considerably, however, when a pair of head-lights appeared at the end of the street. The car was three blocks down to his right and approaching fast. He didn't think the driv-er would spot him, but it wouldn't do to drag his heels.

He got to the hedges at the front of the house by the time the car was a block away and ducked down behind them, remaining there until he saw the taillights recede at the other end of the street. Sighing in relief, he got up and eased himself out from behind the hedges. Some sticky burrs and hard little leaves ad-hered to his clothing and he plucked a few of them away as he moved down along the side of the house. Like his own back yard, this one was encircled by a tall privacy fence. He opened the gate and entered the yard, pulling the gate most of the way closed behind him without latching it.

The shed was in a corner at the back of the yard, which was approximately half the size of Pete's back yard, a consequence of the way the property lines were set along the neighboring streets and alleys. He started moving across the yard and gasped softly in surprise when a light came on at the back of the house. For a moment, he didn't move, frozen in place by shock. Some moments elapsed and he realized all that had happened was he'd triggered a motion sensor. No one was alive in the house, so it didn't matter. He started across the yard again when the light went out.

An initial groan of despair came to his lips as he arrived at the shed and glimpsed the padlock dangling from the hasp. Despair gave way to relief in the next instant, however, when he realized the lock was hanging open. The shackle had not been clicked into place. He sighed in relief, slipped the shackle free of the hasp, and tossed the padlock aside. It landed with an audible thump on the ground somewhere nearby.

The hinges on the shed's door creaked as Pete pulled it open, making him wince until he again belatedly remembered he was the only one around to hear it. Once the door was all the way open, he stepped into the shed and felt around until he found a light switch. He flipped the switch and squinted against the sudden glare dispersing the darkness.

A big work table took up much of the space. Various tools and boxes were piled atop it. Stowed beneath the table was a push mower and a rusting tricycle. The item he needed was hanging from a peg on one of the walls. He maneuvered around the table and took the long-handled axe down from its peg. It had a solid, heavy feel to it. He put the ball of a thumb to the blade, gingerly testing it for sharpness. Even this slight amount of pressure produced a shallow, bloodless slice in his skin. He jerked the thumb away before the bloodless part of that could change. The axe was plenty sharp enough. If he couldn't dismember dead woman number one's body with this thing, he wouldn't be able to do it at all.

Pete was starting to make his way back around the table when he spied a chainsaw resting on a bench. It looked like one of the gas-powered ones rather than an electric model. A gas can sat next to it on the bench. He hesitated before continuing on out of the shed, contemplating the possibilities of the chainsaw. It would make the nasty job ahead of him much easier. The big blade would be able to chew quickly through muscle, bone, and sinew. He could be done dismembering the corpse within minutes, as opposed to strenuously hacking and hacking away with the axe. It was going to be a nasty, messy job no matter how he went about it. Speeding the process up considerably would be a wonderful thing. On the other hand, taking a corpse apart with a chainsaw would be far noisier than doing it with an axe. He imagined people walking by in the street and hearing a chainsaw running in his house. Maybe they'd think nothing of it. Maybe they'd think he was watching a scary movie on a loud surround system.

Or maybe not.

Maybe they'd hear it and call the police right away.

Another thing to consider, concealing an axe when he crossed the street again would be a far easier thing than concealing a chainsaw. He could jam the axe-head up under his armpit and hold the handle stiffly at his side as he hurried across the street.

He sighed.

Okay, the axe it is.

He'd just flipped off the light switch and was about to step out of the shed when the phone in his pocket rang. Frowning, he took the phone out and squinted at the screen. It was Mary.

He answered and put the phone to his ear. "What?"

"Stop rooting around out there and come into the house."

"Um ..."

She grunted. "Yes, I'm in your neighbors' house. I saw you come out of your house and cross the street. Then I saw you go in the back yard. What are you doing out there anyway?"

"Um ..."

"Never mind. Just come into the house through the back. It's not locked."

She hung up.

Pete put the phone away and hesitated a moment longer, wondering if he should return the axe to its peg or take it with him.

He opted for the latter.

FIFTEEN

A set of sliding glass doors overlooked a patio at the back of the house. Pete rolled the door open and stepped into a large dining room, a gauzy curtain billowing in the breeze as he entered the house. There were no lights on in the house. Leaving the sliding door open, he moved carefully through the dark dining room, seeing the faint outline of an archway to his left and another one right in front of him. The one in front of him was much wider and on the opposite side of a big round dining table.

A woman was seated in a chair at the dining table. She was facing away from Pete as he moved closer to the table and tightened his grip on the axe handle. He began to lift the axe, consumed with the sudden urge to put an abrupt end to this madness. Killing a person was something he would have found unimaginable before today, but he had a different view of the matter now. This woman had set horrendous things in motion and was responsible for the deaths of several people. Even if she hadn't killed them with her own hands, their murders had happened at her bidding. She deserved retribution. Also, if he killed her now, he might be able to locate her phone and scrub it of any incriminating information. He became almost giddy at the thought. The possibility of getting free of what had seemed an impossible situation suddenly felt within his grasp.

Before he could get the axe lifted above his head, however, he noted the slouched position of the woman in the chair. Other things were off as well. Her head was lolling to one side. The woman's wavy hair was blonde like Mary's and in the dark appeared similarly styled, but now he saw it was much shorter.

"That's not me, you idiot."

Pete gasped and glanced in the direction of the wider archway. The slim, shadowy shape of a woman appeared. As Pete eyed the form warily, he heard the sound of a thumb flicking at a lighter. A thin column of orange flame appeared in the darkness. She lit a cigarette and put the lighter away.

"Come in here with me, Pete. Let's talk."

She turned away from him and disappeared into the deeper shadows beyond the archway. Pete did not immediately follow her into whatever room she had entered. Instead, he moved around the table until he had an unobstructed view of the woman sitting slumped in the chair. He pulled out his phone again and used the light of the screen to see her better. He grimaced, seeing the deep slash wound to her throat. Gouts of blood had left the front of her body coated in crimson. The dead woman was Stan's wife, Linda. He took a closer look around the dining room and saw no sign of the murdered couple's daughter, but he was sure her corpse was somewhere else in the house.

He followed Mary through the wide archway into what he was able to discern as a large living room even in the inky darkness. Mary had taken a seat at one end of a long sectional. Pete saw the glowing tip of her cigarette rise in the darkness and burn brighter for a moment as she inhaled from it. As he inched closer—moving slowly to avoid unseen obstructions—she leaned forward and stubbed her cigarette out in an ashtray. He edged around a coffee table and in another moment stood no more than five feet directly in front of her. His hand again tightened around the axe handle.

"That's close enough," she told him.

There was a click and then Pete was squinting against the glare of a lamp, which was on a little round side table at the end of the sectional. A gun was clutched in Mary's right hand. A little revolver. The barrel was aimed directly at his abdomen.

She smiled. "Put the axe down if you don't want to get shot."

Pete tossed the axe aside. It landed with a muffled thump on the carpeted floor. "I'll need to take it with me when I leave."

Mary had changed out of her professional attire since the last time Pete had seen her, much earlier in the day. Gone were the pencil skirt, fitted pinstriped top, and heels. Now she was wearing a pair of dark blue sneakers, tight black leggings, and a loose black sweatshirt. Pete immediately understood the practical reason for the change. These were clothes for prowling around in the night.

She gestured with the cigarette. "And why would you need an axe, Pete?"

"Because hacking up that poor woman's body into manageable pieces is the only feasible way to accomplish the latest fucked-up task you've assigned me."

She frowned, shaking her head. "Hmm, no, that's not what I want. If I'd wanted you to dismember a corpse, I would have said so. I'm afraid you'll have to bring her over here in one piece."

Pete made a sound of deep exasperation. "There's no way I can do that without someone seeing me."

She shrugged. "Well, Pete, you better find a way. My game, my rules." She stood up and slowly approached him, keeping the barrel of the gun aimed squarely at his midsection. "You have just two other options. One, you can quit the game, at which point I'll have no choice but to start posting those photos. Or ..." She smiled as she came closer still and pressed the gun's barrel against his stomach, pushing it in hard enough to hurt. "If you feel you can't live with the shame and consequences of what you've done, I can just kill you now. In your place, I would seriously consider picking that option. You'd be dead, but you'd be spared the messy aftermath. Make up your mind, Pete. Keep playing or don't. You have ten seconds until I decide for you. One, two, three, four—"

The rapid way she rattled off the numbers sent a jolt of terror through Pete. "Stop! I'll keep playing. Jesus."

She made a sound of mock disappointment and arranged her features in an exaggerated frown. "Aw, I was sort of hoping you'd choose that last option. Killing you has never been the ultimate goal of the game, but I have to admit I'd find satisfaction in watching you die." The gun was still wedged against his stomach and now she dug it in a little deeper, making him wince. "I'd shoot you once right through here rather than doing the standard double-tap to the back of the head. Then I'd sit down, smoke another cigarette, and listen to you moan and cry while you bleed out on the floor. I think I'd really enjoy that."

Pete started trembling again as she talked about shooting him. He didn't think she would do it, at least not yet, but the hard steel pressing into him made it difficult to take that for granted. He sniffled. "Please don't."

She reached up to lightly stroke one side of his face with her fingertips. "You poor thing. You're so frightened. Like a little child afraid of the boogeyman. Only you're a grown man, sort of, which makes it extra pathetic. Wouldn't you agree?"

Pete sniffled again and said nothing.

Mary's fingernails began to dig into his cheek. "Answer me. Wouldn't you agree?"

Pete choked back a sob and nodded. "Yes. I ... agree."

Mary smiled and her hand came away from his face. Little beads of blood welled up from two of the deeper indentations her nails had made. "Good. Now, here's what happens next. Go back to your house and get the girl. Bring her over here and put her in the crawlspace like I told you in the first fucking place. In one goddamn piece. I don't care how you do it, just do it. You'll have ten minutes to get it done starting as soon as you leave by the front door. When it's done, text me a picture of the bitch in the crawlspace as proof. If I don't get that picture by the time your ten minutes is up, I start posting those other photos. I won't be here by the time you return and neither will that axe so get any ideas of turning things around on me out of your stupid fucking skull. Got it?"

He frowned. "I don't think I should risk being seen going out the front way. Bringing her in through the back would—"

She took the gun away from his abdomen and smacked the butt of it against the side of his head, making him take a few staggering steps sideways. "Don't argue with me. Do exactly as you're told or eat a fucking bullet. Up to you."

Pete gingerly touched the aching side of his head and whimpered.

Mary aimed the gun at him again, this time at the middle of his face. "Go, Pete."

He nodded and turned away from her, leaving the house through the front door without another word.

SIXTEEN

A car turned down the street in the same moment Pete stepped out onto the porch. He debated staying where he was until the driver either parked the car somewhere on the street or drove on by, but the car was moving slowly and Pete was conscious of the necessity of working quickly. His allotted ten minutes had already started and were ticking by quickly. Muttering a curse under his breath, he stepped down from the porch and began to hurry across the lawn. He was at the edge of the lawn when the car abruptly sped up and came to a squealing stop in the middle of the street, blocking his way.

The window on the passenger side of the old, maroon-colored Tercel slid down and the pudgy face of a rotund and rosy-cheeked young man peered out at him. His spiky hair had an excessive amount of product in it. "Hey, dude, you know how to get to the stadium from here?"

Pete knew how to get to the stadium, but giving directions would cost him more time than he could afford. Even asking the fat guy why he didn't just use GPS was problematic, as it would come with the risk of opening up a prolonged line of conversation. Being rude was something he always tried to avoid, even when doing so was the easiest way out of an uncomfortable encounter.

He shook his head and said, in as emphatic a tone as he could manage, "No."

The big man frowned and tilted his head, glancing at the house behind Pete. "Man, don't you live around here?"

Pete simply repeated what he'd already said: "No."

The driver, who looked like a thinner version of the guy who'd first addressed Pete, sighed in exasperation. "Fuck it, man. Dude's an asshole. We'll ask somebody else."

The big man in the passenger seat sneered. "Thanks for nothing, dick."

In his lap was one of those enormous fountain drinks sold at convenience stores. The big man removed the top and tossed the plastic cup out the window at Pete. The contents of the cup soaked the front of his shirt as the cup hit him and fell to the street. He heard the laughter of the young men trailing out of the car's open window as they sped away.

Pete stood there in disbelief for a moment, plucking the wet front of his shirt away from his skin. "Jesus. Fucking assholes."

This just wasn't his day on any level whatsoever. He felt

cursed.

He hurried on across the street and raced across his own lawn, vaulting up the steps to the porch and hauling the door open. As soon as he was inside, he stopped cold and put a hand to his mouth, his face twisting in disgust. Shane Watson had again entered the house during his absence. He was naked now, his discarded clothes in a haphazard pile by the coffee table. It wasn't Shane's nudity that bothered him, though, but rather what he was doing. He was on top of dead woman number two, rutting away between her spread legs. Her black panties had been stripped away and tossed aside.

Pete took the hand away from his mouth. "What the fuck are you doing? What's wrong with you?"

Shane glanced up at him, pausing only slightly in his rutting. "Hey, don't judge me, man. I'm not doing this because I want to. The evil cunt told me to do it. I don't have a fucking choice. Don't believe me? Look over there."

Shane jerked his chin in the direction of the coffee table.

Pete followed his gaze and saw that Mary was monitoring the act of necrophilia on her iPhone via Facetime. It was initially hard to tell from the angle of her phone's camera, but she appeared to be inside a car.

She smiled when she saw Pete looking. "Hi, Pete. You better get cracking. Time's running out."

Pete groaned and ran a hand through his hair. "Please just give me another few minutes. I got delayed by some assholes asking for directions."

Mary made a tsk-tsk sound and shook her head. "Not my problem. You've got less than seven minutes."

"Fuck!"

There was no point in any further pleading for leniency. She clearly wasn't interested in cutting him even the slightest slack. Moving with as much speed as he could manage, he hopped over Shane and the dead woman and shoved the coffee table aside. The iPhone had been propped up against the black gift box, but now it fell over. He doubted Mary would be pleased about that, but he needed room to operate. Grabbing hold of dead woman number one by the ankles, he summoned as much strength as he could manage and hauled her off the couch, grimacing when the back of her head hit the hardwood floor with a sickening crack. He dragged her around the prone forms of Shane and the blonde corpse, grunting and straining as rivulets of sweat began to slide down the side of his head.

By the time he maneuvered her over to the door, opened it again, and got ready to drag her outside, it felt as if multiple more minutes had already passed. The task was feeling more impossible than ever. A crazy idea occurred to him. Maybe he should get in his car and drive away from all this, go somewhere far, far away and start over with a new identity. Crazy though it clearly was, he was momentarily tempted by the idea. The only problem was he didn't have the first clue how to go about successfully crafting a new identity for himself. He wasn't a professional criminal. The police would track him down, he was sure of it.

Then he thought of another crazy idea.

An even crazier one, actually.

The car.

The idea was beyond insane, but it might be the only way he could get this done in the time remaining to him. He dragged his keys out of his pocket, dashed outside, and got in his car. After jamming the key in the ignition and starting the engine, he put the car in gear, hit the gas, and sped across his lawn until his front bumper bumped against the bottom step of the porch. He wrenched the gearshift over to P and left the motor running as he got out of the car. Next he opened the screen door and set the sliding clasp at the top to hold it open. He then grabbed dead woman number one by the ankles again and dragged the body across the porch and then onto the hood of his car.

The heels of his shoes made slight metallic crumpling sounds as he maneuvered the body around on the hood, arranging it so it was sprawled lengthwise in front of the windshield. He wished he had a rope or something he could use to strap the body down, but he didn't and there wasn't time anyway. He'd just have to hope the corpse wouldn't go slewing away to the ground as he got the car turned around and pointed toward the house across the street.

Then it hit him—why even bother with that?

He jumped down from the hood and began to get back in the car. Before he could drop in behind the wheel, he heard Shane shout at him, "You're a crazy motherfucker, Adler!"

Pete almost grinned at the comment.

Takes one to know one.

He got in behind the wheel, hit the button to roll his window down, and reached out to take hold of the woman by an arm. This might not do any good, but it was better than nothing. He put the car in reverse and hit the gas again. The car sped backward across his lawn, bumped jarringly as it hit the street, then bumped again upon reaching the opposite lawn. He did this without any regard for anyone who might be watching or any possible oncoming traffic. Things had reached a desperate point. All he could do was act and hope for the best.

The bumps did jostle the corpse, the other end of which began to slew toward the center of the hood. However, he was able to maintain his grip on the dead woman's arm and thus keep her from sliding off. When he was almost all the way to poor, dead Stan Richardson's porch, he maneuvered the car in a sort of half-loop over the remaining distance, cutting the wheel hard as he came to an abrupt stop parallel to the porch. This final maneuver was executed with enough momentum to send the body flying off the hood and onto the porch.

He heard someone call out, "Holy shit! Touchdown!"

His heart almost stopped at hearing these words. Then his head snapped back toward his house and he saw Shane Watson on the porch. He had his hands upraised in the manner of a football referee signaling a touchdown and was doing a goofy little circular dance on the porch. Then he stopped and pointed across the street, raising a thumb to signal either admiration or approval. Or both. The inadvisability of both the ridiculous display and the loud exclamation was obvious, but he couldn't take the time to admonish Shane. Besides, the maneuver *had* kind of merited it.

Throwing open the car door, he got out, hopped up onto the porch, and grabbed hold of the dead woman's ankles again. He took a quick look around and saw no one other than Shane watching him, though there were headlights again at the far end of the street. His heart pumping so loud the beats sounded like amplified bass drums, he nudged the partly open door the rest of the way open and hurriedly dragged the body into the house. He got the front door shut in the last instant before the car drew abreast of the house and drove on by.

Helpfully, the lamp was still on in the living room. Twisting his head rapidly around, he was able to locate the likely main hallway entrance. Grunting and straining again, he dragged the body in that direction. He moved fast and without much care, causing the woman's head to bang against the corner as he pulled her into the hallway. He twisted his head around again as he made himself keep moving, spying the closet at the far end of the hallway. Sweat dripped from seemingly every pore in his body as he closed the remaining distance faster than he ever could have imagined. He was hauling a significant amount of weight around like a longshoreman or something, which was probably only possible due to the massive amount of adrenaline currently racing through his system.

Once he reached the closet, he let go of the dead woman's ankles and the heels of her feet thumped on the hardwood floor. He opened the closet and saw the crawlspace door at the back. A vacuum cleaner was in the way. He pulled it out and tossed it down the hallway. It landed with a loud clatter, pieces of it breaking off and spinning away on the floor.

Crouching down, he leaned inside and pulled at the door, encountering stiff resistance at first that made him whine in frustration. He kept at it, though, bearing down with all his might until the door abruptly slid all the way open. A glance into the dark space revealed that another body had already been shoved in there. He couldn't see the face, but judging by the shape of the nude form, he surmised it was likely Stan and Linda Richardson's dead daughter. This was irritating at first, but another moment's inspection left him pretty sure there was room for the dead stripper in there, too.

Almost done, he thought, panting heavily. *Just get her the fuck in there.*

And that was what he did.

SEVENTEEN

Getting the second body jammed in there wasn't easy. By the time he was finished, the corpses were packed into the crawlspace like sardines. Fitting anything else in there larger than the size of, say, a can of beer would have been impossible. He didn't care, though, because he *had* gotten it done, which was all that mattered.

He took out his phone and squatted just inside the closet as he aimed the phone at the open crawlspace, tapping the flash button before taking a picture so the image would be clear. After snapping the picture, he backed out of the closet and got to his feet. He inserted the image in a text to Mary and hit the send button.

Less than a minute later, notification of an incoming Facetime call appeared on the screen. He accepted the call and

Mary's image appeared. She was still behind the wheel of a car, probably parked somewhere nearby, though again it was hard to tell much from the angle and close-up view of her face.

"Hello, Pete," she said, flashing a big smile worthy of a swimsuit model in a tanning lotion ad. In Pete's opinion, she looked far too happy for someone who'd spent the day orchestrating a series of gruesome murders. "I see you were able to deliver the package to the designated location. Congratulations on a job well done." Now the smile faded and her expression took on the stern aspect of a frustrated teacher admonishing one of her slower students. "Unfortunately, you failed to complete the task within the time frame allowed. I didn't receive photographic confirmation until just over four minutes after time was up. And you know what that means."

Pete groaned. "Oh, come the fuck on! That's not my fault. Please don't punish me for getting waylaid by those assholes asking for directions."

Mary's stern expression remained in place a stomach-churning moment longer, then it softened again and she laughed. "Relax, Pete. Performing these tasks in the prescribed way and within any constraints I place on you is important. In this one case, however, I've decided to cut you some slack. After hearing Shane's account of how you delivered the package, I'm awarding you some bonus points for creativity and, frankly, for showing some fucking balls for once in your life. I won't post the incriminating images to the PD's Facebook page." Her smile shifted, becoming a smirk. "At least not yet."

Pete let out a relieved breath and put his back to one of the walls in the hallway. The adrenaline burst that had been driving him for the last several minutes was fading. He felt an overwhelming weariness in every part of his body. It was tempting to just slide to the floor, close his eyes, and take a nap right here in the hallway. He cleared his throat and said, "Is the game over yet? Because I have to tell you, I'm already at the limit of what I can take. Beyond, maybe."

Mary shook her head. "Not quite yet. There's still one other package in need of being rerouted to a new location." She chuckled. "I'm sure you get my drift. Oh, don't look so upset. I'm going to allow you some time to rest and get your energy back up for the final phase of this thing. You have an hour to spend in whatever way you wish until I contact you again with your next set of instructions."

Frowning, Pete pushed away from the wall. "You said 'final phase'. Will this next thing really be the end of it? Because I wasn't lying about being at the end of my rope. There's not much more I can take."

She nodded. "Yes, Pete. The next part is the last part. You have my word on that."

Her image vanished as she ended the Facetime call. Pete dropped the phone back in his pocket and walked out of the hallway, pausing long enough in the living room to verify the axe was no longer there. It was gone, just as Mary had said it would be. He thought about the chainsaw still out there in the shed and considered taking the time to retrieve it, but ultimately decided against it. He couldn't imagine effectively wielding it as a weapon. Mary was too careful and tricky about everything, controlling the situation at every step. The gun she'd pulled on him was evidence of that. She would never allow herself to be in a truly vulnerable position. And with corpse dismemberment being forbidden under the rules of her game, he no longer needed it for any other reason.

Pete went to the front door and cracked it open just enough for a peek outside. His car was right where he'd left it, parked alongside the porch. He opened the door a little wider and saw that no one was out in the street gawking at it. Slipping out of the house, he eased the door shut, but left it unlocked. If he managed to survive Mary's game, it might become necessary to return before sunrise and do some cleanup work. He would at least need to wipe down every surface he might have touched. Or, and this idea occurred to him as he was stepping down from the porch, he could soak the interior of the house in kerosene and just set the damn thing on fire. Complete obliteration of the place might be the surest method of eliminating anything incriminating.

His car's engine was still running as Pete slid in behind the wheel. After changing gears, he steered the car back across the street and into his driveway, cutting the engine as soon as he'd come to a stop. He got out and took a look around. There were still no signs that anyone other than Shane had observed his lunatic stunt, which he could only ascribe to sheer luck. He had a hunch he would need a lot more blind luck to have any hope of surviving Mary's game without winding up dead or in jail. What scared him was the possibility he'd already used up the last bit of luck the universe would allow him for one night. He hoped the last part of the game wouldn't involve risk of public exposure, because he strongly sensed he wouldn't get away with something like what he'd just done a second time in one night.

Shane was gone by the time he got back inside the house, but evidence of the vile act he'd performed was still on display. The discarded panties and the splayed legs of the corpse, now stiff and discolored from rigor mortis. A significant amount of a white, thickly creamy substance oozed from the dead woman's vagina. Pete's stomach churned at the thought that this was Shane's semen, because if it was, the man had to be infested with every venereal disease known to man. Glimpsing something in his peripheral vision, Pete turned and saw a jar sitting on one of his bookshelves.

Shane had used mayonnaise from his fridge as lube. His gaze lingered on the nearly empty jar many seconds longer than necessary. It was just a jar. An innocent inanimate object. As he stared almost numbly at it, there was no conscious contemplation of the act the substance it contained had been used to facilitate. Beneath the surface, however, something was happening, a primordial reaction that first manifested in the form of a burp. More gaseous disturbances brought a sour feeling to his stomach and made the muscles of his throat work in an ominous way that heralded an eruption far more severe than a mere burp.

His face was covered in sweat. He felt woozy.

"Oh, god ..."

After another, louder burp, he abruptly raced into the bathroom, dropped to his knees in front of the toilet, raised the toilet seat, and leaned forward as his mouth opened wide to unleash a stream of vomit. The ejected contents of his stomach hit the water in the bowl with enough force to spatter his face with droplets of vomit-tainted moisture, some of which went right into his open mouth. He had time enough to whimper miserably before his stomach heaved again with seemingly even more force, though significantly less actual bile was expelled this time. That was the worst of it, but the heaving continued for several more minutes before his stomach muscles at last began to relax.

After reaching up to grab the flush handle and push it down with an unsteady hand, he slammed the toilet seat down and got shakily to his feet. He lurched over to the wash basin, braced his hands against its edge, and raised his head to study his reflection in the mirror above the sink. He was red-faced and sweaty. His jaw was quivering and his face was spattered with tiny bits of partially digested food remnants.

Pete grimaced. "Gross."

He turned on the water and grabbed a hand towel from a ring mounted on the wall by the door. After cleaning his face as thoroughly as possible, he still felt shaky, but a little better overall. He turned off the water and left the soiled hand towel on the edge of the basin as he staggered out of the bathroom and into his bedroom. His T-shirt was still soaked from having the giant soda cup tossed at him. He stripped it off and proceeded to remove the rest of his clothes, dropping them in the laundry basket at the foot of his bed. An impulse led him back into the bathroom, where he turned on the shower and stepped beneath the nozzle after allowing the water a moment to heat up.

On one level, he knew that by doing this he was temporarily making himself even more vulnerable than he already was. It was impossible to stand vigilant against household intruders while naked in the shower. The possibility of either Shane or Mary entering his house again under these circumstances did cause a flicker of concern, but not enough to matter. Mary had promised him an hour before the next phase of the game commenced. Yes, promises didn't mean much coming from someone like her, but he figured he would take his chances anyway. He was close to the point of not giving a shit anymore. Maybe one of them would come into his house again and maybe not. Either way, it wasn't like he'd be able to stop them. Calling the alarm company to change his security code might have been an option earlier in the day, before things really got out of hand, but it wasn't one anymore. There was no point. If he changed the code and one of those loons triggered the alarm, it would result in a visit by the cops, something not even the tiniest little part of him still wanted.

Meanwhile, he felt contaminated by the vile deeds he'd been forced to participate in throughout the day—as well as by the many other horrible things he'd seen—and was now consumed with a primal need to cleanse himself. He would be forced to again do more revolting, messy things before the end of the night. No doubt about it. Before that happened, though, he could at least feel like himself again for a while.

Once he'd scrubbed every inch of his body as thoroughly as he could manage, he stood beneath the hot water stream a minute longer, allowing himself the illusion that the water was purifying him. He cut the water when it began to turn lukewarm and got out, the old metal curtain rings softly squealing as they slid along the shower rod. He toweled off and returned to the bedroom, feeling much steadier on his feet as he began to dress himself, selecting a pair of dark-colored jeans and a plain black T-shirt, clothes that felt like the right choice in the event he was again forced to do anything shady outside.

After he was dressed, he wandered back out to the living room and again took in the scene of carnage and madness, this time without even the smallest quiver of nausea. He was past the primal shock of it, it seemed. Instead, he catalogued it all in an almost dispassionate way. It was mildly dismaying to learn how quickly a person could become inured to the most horrendous things, but even that seemed of little consequence at this point. That all these innocent people had lost their lives was unfortunate, but even that injustice didn't matter to him much now. He just wanted to get through this somehow.

It became a mantra in his head.

I just want to get through this. I just want to get through this. I just want to get through this. Please let me come out of this okay. Please ...

By his estimate, he still had roughly another half hour before Mary called him again. He decided it'd be smart to fill that time by at least beginning to take some kind of positive action, which did not include getting into the beer again. What was left of his twelve-pack was still on the coffee table. It appeared Shane had helped himself to a few in Pete's absence. He didn't care. Trying to get drunk had been a badly misguided idea from the start. Now that any trace of his buzz had faded, this felt painfully clear. The stress had driven him to it.

Pete went into the kitchen and grabbed two large black garbage bags from the pantry, as well as a pair of yellow rubber dishwashing gloves from under the sink. He took the bags and the gloves out to the living room, dropped one bag on the coffee table, and shook the other one open. Ridding his house fully of the horrors on display was the ultimate goal. Might as well start now while he had some time to kill. After donning the gloves, he went to work.

Stan Richardson's head and the plush gift box in which it rested were the first things to go in the bag. He couldn't help feeling a faint echo of his previous queasiness, especially when he felt the heaviness of the severed head dragging down the bag as he moved about the room. The severed tongue and the mayonnaise jar also went in the bag, along with the handbags that had belonged to the dead strippers. Any impulse to sort through their belongings was gone. He was thinking of them as objects now and had no desire to re-humanize them. Remembering the penis sitting in a Tupperware container on his stove, he made a detour into the kitchen, where he resealed the container and dropped it in the bag. He returned to the living room and surveyed it again to see if he'd missed anything. Spying dead woman number two's discarded panties, he knelt to retrieve them with the intention of also dropping them in the bag. He decided against it, figuring he might want to slide them back into place on the woman's body.

After tying up the bag and leaving it on the kitchen floor for later disposal, Pete took a glass down from his cupboard, filled it with ice cubes and water, and carried it out to the living room. He settled into the recliner, heaved a tired sigh, and sipped water as he rested and awaited Mary's call.

EIGHTEEN

Pete was dozing off when he dimly perceived his phone's ringtone emanating from his hip pocket. The nearly empty glass of ice water was still loosely clasped in his fingers. He set the glass on the floor and dragged out his phone.

Mary's name was on the screen. He hadn't expected to see anything else, of course. Not many people intentionally put in a call to his number these days. Multiple robocalls came in daily, of course, but calls from real people were a rarity. It was a sad state of affairs, he supposed. Hardly anyone wanted anything to do with him. Any other night, contemplation of this reality might have sent him spiraling into depression, but tonight it wasn't one of his bigger concerns. He accepted the call and put the phone to his ear. "Hello, Mary."

"Hello, you squirmy little maggot-thing." She laughed, a

sound echoed by someone sitting near her. The other person's laughter had a distinctly masculine tinge to it. Shane, probably. Pete pictured the corpse-fucker seated in the passenger seat of the car he'd glimpsed in the Facetime calls earlier. A car he belatedly realized wasn't the same car Mary had been driving the whole time he'd known her. The upholstery was a much darker gray. "Are you ready to start the last part of the game?"

"Yeah. I'm ready."

A disappointed-sounding grunt came from the other end. "What, no snappy comeback? No profane insinuations regarding the state of my mental health?"

"Not in the mood. Sorry."

Mary sighed. "Oh, that's too bad. I must admit, I was pleasantly surprised by your outbursts earlier in the evening. I know I said all I wanted from you was obsequiousness, but the angry banter was kind of fun. Ah, well." Another sigh. "I suppose there's no point delaying things further, anyway. I do have a schedule of my own to keep, believe it or not, and there's little room for additional fooling around. I'll text you an address when I end this call. You will have one hour from the time you receive the text to transport the other package to that address."

"By 'other package', I'm guessing you mean the other dead stripper."

Mary laughed. "Dead stripper. How funny. You're such a joker, Pete." The phony humor faded from her voice with her next words. "You know very well what I mean. Deliver the package to the designated location within the time allowed or else. And you know exactly what that means, too."

Pete grimaced. "Yeah. I know what it fucking means."

"Good. I do have some additional requirements for transportation of the package. I'm afraid you're not going to like them." A faint sound of laughter from Mary's male companion followed this declaration. Mary did not react, at least not in a way that came through on the phone. "Your inclination will be to transport the package in the trunk of your car. This will not be allowed. Instead, the package should ride next to you on the front passenger seat. Do nothing to obscure the nature of the package. If you violate these rules, you will pay a steep price. The loss of your freedom, for certain. It might even cost you your life." She forced a laugh. "Figuratively speaking, of course. This is just a fun game. Isn't it, Pete?"

There was a harder edge in her voice as she spoke those last few words. Pete felt dismay at the requirements she'd imposed for this supposed last stage of the game, but he had no interest in agitating her any further.

"That's right. It's just a game."

A long sigh from the other end. "I'm glad we understand each other. Remember, follow the rules and all will be well. You may be tempted to skirt the rules by transporting the package in your trunk until you are nearly to your destination. That would be a mistake. You are still being monitored. Goodbye, Pete. I'm hanging up now. And good luck."

The line went dead. The tone signaling the arrival of a new text sounded just as Pete was taking the phone away from his ear. As promised, there was an address in the message. It was not an address Pete recognized, but the zip code told him it was not inside the city limits. This was confirmed when he entered the address in Google search, which helpfully brought up directions and a map. It was a business address, for a storage facility in a little town one county over.

Pete began to feel anxious again as he started to think about the logistics of completing this supposed last part of the game. The address was farther away than he would have liked, but getting there within the prescribed time was not out of the question now that it was much later at night. And once he got out on the highway, he'd be able to make up some time by speeding ... Not too much, though. Cops would be on the lookout for drunk drivers, same as every weekend, but he thought he'd probably be fine going ten to fifteen miles over the posted speed limit, especially if he could manage to stay within the yellow lines and not weave around like a drunkard. Being totally sober now, that shouldn't be an issue.

More troublesome than the time issue was the necessity of transporting dead woman number two in the way he'd been instructed. The distance involved was significant, slightly over twenty miles. A long way to ride with a corpse sitting in the passenger seat of his car. The risk of being spotted and pulled over by police was high. The one thing working in his favor was that it was nighttime. People speeding by on the interstate wouldn't be able to see her clearly, anyway. And if he positioned the body in just the right way, it might appear as if the dead woman was merely taking a nap.

Pete nodded as he thought about it, his shaky confidence growing slightly. It was a hugely risky proposition any way you looked at it, but it might just be doable. He looked at dead woman number two. "Okay, let's do this thing."

The corpse, of course, did not respond.

Pete frowned as he stared at her stiffly splayed legs. He pulled up Google on his phone again and did some quick research on rigor mortis. While he believed the corpse might be passable as a napping woman in the correct pose, her current state would not be conducive to conveying such an impression. He grimaced and shook his head as he skimmed through a lengthy article regarding post-mortem handling of corpses at morgues.

He put the phone away and went to work stretching the dead woman's legs out to break the rigor mortis. This was not easy. Sweat formed on his brow again as he grunted and strained. Handling a corpse again was not pleasant, of course, but he'd already done that plenty today and thus intimately handling dead flesh was not the most upsetting aspect of what he was doing. He was a lot more bothered by how much time it was eating up. At last, however, he was able to render her stiffened limbs pliable enough for transport.

A peek outside revealed a street currently free of pedestrian and automotive traffic. It was getting late enough now that there should be significantly fewer cars moving through the area. Didn't mean one wouldn't come along at the wrong time, just that the risk was lower.

He grabbed his keys and went outside, dashing over to his car and slipping in behind the wheel within just a few seconds. More cognizant than ever of the need to make up time, he was moving as quickly as he could manage without tripping over his feet. He started the car and steered it across the lawn, pulling up alongside the porch with the passenger door facing the steps. On the verge of getting out, he thought of something and took a moment to pop the trunk. Then he got out and hurried around to the other side of the car, pulling the passenger side door open as far as it would go. Next he raced back up the steps, opened the screen door, and set it so it would stay open.

Back inside the house, he grabbed the dead woman under the arms and grunted as he dragged her over to the threshold. He paused there to take another look outside. The street was still empty. He resumed dragging the corpse across the porch and then down the steps, heaving her up once he reached the sidewalk in preparation of dumping her into the passenger seat. Before he could do that, however, headlights appeared in the street to his right, barely more than a block away and closing fast.

Shit!

Not knowing what else to do, Pete hugged the corpse tightly against him, encircling it in a way he hoped would look like a loving embrace. The dead woman's recently manipulated arms flopped loosely at her sides. Pete put his chin in the crook of her neck and held on as the car came closer. The brown Toyota Camry slowed slightly as it neared his house. Pete couldn't see the driver from this angle, but the Camry's windows were down and he heard laughter emanating from inside it.

Someone in the car yelled, "Drunk bitch!"

More laughter. Sounded like teenagers.

Then the car's tires squealed as the driver hit the gas and sped away.

Pete let out a relieved breath.

He eased the dead woman into the passenger seat somewhat more delicately than he'd originally intended, some instinct making him want to treat her with more respect than the kids in the Camry. After taking a couple extra minutes to arrange the corpse in the napping pose, he eased the passenger door shut and rushed back into the house to grab the garbage bag and lock up the house. Before leaving again, he paused as he thought of one more item he wanted to take with him.

In a drawer in the kitchen—along with numerous other odds and ends—was a folding knife with a black handle. The blade was a big one, sharp and with some real heft to it. Taking it with him was probably a useless gesture. He might not see Mary again tonight. Or ever. She had a gun, though. He knew that. And taking along some kind of weapon wasn't the worst idea ever, even if it was highly unlikely he'd have to use it.

Pete went back outside.

After closing and locking the front door, he hurried down the steps and dropped the garbage bag in the trunk. A few seconds later, he was behind the wheel of his car and driving away from his house.

NINETEEN

On his way out to the interstate, Pete encountered some maddeningly slow stop-and-start traffic, a problem that steadily worsened the closer he got to the nearest interstate junction. This was annoying, but not unexpected, given the proximity of his neighborhood to the downtown area. Traffic was lighter on his own street at this later hour, but this was still the weekend. Downtown would remain alive with drunken revelry for hours to come, which meant a high volume of cars cycling in and out of the city at all times.

Pete watched the light at the exit he needed to take cycle through the green-yellow-red pattern a dozen times as the traffic in front of him inched slowly forward. While he waited in helpless frustration, Pete repeatedly glanced at the dashboard clock, willing the maddeningly fast passage of minutes to slow down.

As the light up ahead began its cycle yet again, he alternately tapped his gas and brake pedals, allowing the car to keep inching forward while his mind wandered. He ruminated some more on his solitary existence, in particular the way it had made this situation so much worse. He had no confidantes, no real close friends. No one who would have his back no matter what and would try to help. His eyes misted as it hit him that this might have been a big factor in why Mary had targeted him. He was just so perfectly vulnerable.

A horn honked somewhere behind Pete, making him flinch.

He sat up straighter in his seat and saw that traffic in front of him had moved forward. There was a gap of approximately two car-lengths ahead of him. A check of his rearview mirror showed more than one vehicle to his rear swerving out into the next lane. These were drivers frustrated by the delay, intent on swooping into that open space. Pete glanced at the dead woman slumped in his passenger seat and knew he couldn't allow that. He pushed the gas pedal to the floor and the car shot forward, quickly closing the gap before anyone could cut in front of him.

The last-second maneuver resulted in more horn-honking as well as quite a few bellowed expressions of rage. After pulling up alongside Pete, a big man in a blue Mustang revved his engine to get his attention. Pete reluctantly glanced that way. The man was leaning out his window and thrusting an upraised middle finger in his direction. Even after all he'd been through tonight, Pete was still very much a man who shied away from moments of angry confrontation. He cringingly mouthed the word "sorry" and shifted his gaze back to the car in front of him, keeping it there until the light changed again and he was able to move up another two car-lengths. It still felt like too much time was passing by, which was making him antsier by the second. The good news was one more change of the light should take him through the intersection and then down the exit ramp to the interstate. From there, it should be relatively smooth sailing the rest of the way.

Feeling slightly more relaxed now, he glanced to his right again and saw that the man in the blue Mustang's attention was still focused in his direction. In another instant, Pete realized that wasn't precisely true. The big man wasn't looking at him. He was looking at the slumped-over woman in his passenger seat, his features arranged in a deeply puzzled expression. When the man did look at Pete again, it was with something more akin to wariness than rage.

Pete gulped.

Uh-oh.

A horn honked behind him again. Pete's head snapped forward. The light had changed again and his path to the interstate ramp was clear. Tires squealed on asphalt as he again stomped on the gas pedal. The car lurched forward and roared through the intersection. He steered his way down the curving ramp and kept accelerating as he neared the highway. His heart hammered as he thought about what he'd seen in that man's eyes. It was a look that had conveyed sudden understanding and a deepening sense of horror.

He knows, he thought. *The motherfucker knows.*

Pete didn't doubt this conclusion for even a second. He felt the truth of it as clearly as he'd ever felt anything. Acceptance of this truth sent his anxiety soaring to uncharted new heights. He pictured the guy taking out his phone and putting in a call to the cops. An APB was possibly minutes away from being issued, and his apprehension would surely follow shortly thereafter. He thumped the base of a fist against his steering wheel rim and screeched in frustration. His breathing quickened to a degree that left him feeling on the verge of hyperventilating.

Then several minutes passed and nothing happened other than the dark highway continuing to unfurl ahead of him. He let out a big breath and felt his iron grip on the steering wheel begin to relax. After another uneventful few minutes elapsed, he shifted around in his seat and checked all his mirrors to further appraise the current situation. As expected, he saw countless sets of headlights zipping through the night across multiple lanes of traffic on both sides of the interstate. For now, though, he saw no indication of the flashing blue of police cruisers.

He supposed it was possible the man in the blue Mustang had been too startled by what he thought he'd seen to take note of important things like the make of his car or his license plate number. The reason for the apparent lack of pursuit by law enforcement could be as simple as that. Or perhaps the man had simply opted not to get involved. Pete leaned toward the latter scenario, as it reflected what he likely would have done in the big man's place. He knew, of course, that some people were made of sterner stuff than he was and wouldn't even have considered taking the coward's way out. Regardless, the possible threat the man had posed seemed to have faded away.

The only thing to do now was get to the storage facility before time ran out. There wasn't much farther to go now. He'd plugged the address into Google Maps and was taking direction from the voice navigator. In just under three more miles, he would take an exit into the town where the storage facility was located. From there, the facility would only be two more miles away. Despite his earlier anxiety about the minutes passing too quickly, he realized getting there in time was still doable. As he'd hoped, he'd made up significant time on the interstate. Deciding to make up just a little more, he increased pressure on the gas pedal, causing the speedometer needle to soar past 90 MPH. He kept it there until the exit came into view on his right, at which point he let up on the gas pedal and started tapping the brake. The brief burst of increased speed had been a calculated risk, but one he'd felt was worth taking to earn another minute of breathing space.

At the end of the exit ramp, he merged onto a two-lane street that took him to a four-way intersection, where he pulled into the far left lane and waited for the light to change. When it did, he took the left turn and hit the gas again. He could feel a psychic weight lifting from him as the car straightened out and began the last stretch of this harrowing journey. It was a weight of the spirit so immense it almost felt like a physical thing. He'd be glad to soon be shed of it entirely.

Less than two miles to go now, he thought. *Fuck, yeah!*

In the next second after this thought flitted through his head, a car that had been sitting parked at the shoulder with its lights off pulled into the street behind him. Its headlights came on as it rushed to catch up.

A spinning blue light appeared atop the car.

TWENTY

Pete gasped in dismay when he glanced at his rearview mirror and saw the spinning blue light. This was followed by a drawn-out, despairing groan. He felt like crying at the unfairness of it all. He'd come so close to completing the insane task he'd been assigned, only to be stopped by some bored small town cop barely more than a mile from his destination.

He tapped his brake and slowed down some, but did not immediately pull over to the side of the road. His options were limited. He could admit that the game was over and pull over now. The law could take over from here and begin the monumental task of sorting it all out. He'd be heading straight to jail, a prospect that still filled him with paralyzing dread, but at least in jail Mary would no longer be able to endlessly fuck with him. The only other thing he could do was hit the gas and make a run for it. He tried to imagine himself successfully evading an increasingly intense level of police pursuit and couldn't do it. They'd catch up to him sooner or later and he might even get himself shot in the process. Pete didn't want to be shot even more than he didn't want to go to jail.

Surrendering to the inevitable, he slowed down some more and pulled over to the side of the road, soon coming to a full stop. He put the car in park, hit the button to lower his window, and shut off the engine.

The other car pulled up behind him, stopping with about a half car-length separating their bumpers. Pete could hear the other car's engine idling. He looked at his rearview mirror and frowned as he stared at the spinning blue light. It was so different from the light bar that stretched across the roof of most police cruisers. This light reminded him of the kind used by plainclothes detectives in old TV cop shows. After taking off in hot pursuit of some bad guy, they'd grab the rotating dome light, reach out the window, and slap the thing down on the roof of their car. Those scenes were always the same. Really dramatic. Pounding but cheesy '70s theme music, usually with a hint of a funky disco beat. Pete couldn't remember the last time he'd seen one of those removable dome lights in real life.

Or if he ever had.

At least another full minute passed before Pete heard the loud creak of a door opening. A portly man in dark clothes got out of the cop car, which Pete now saw had no markings or emblems of any kind. In Pete's mind, that about sealed it. This was a plainclothes cop he was dealing with, no mere patrol officer. His dread of what the cop was about to discover in his car was still there, but now he felt a little flicker of excitement. This cop being a detective might work to his benefit. A detective wouldn't just take things at face value. He would listen to Pete's wild story and logically puzzle the whole thing out. He would see that Pete was a pitiful stooge callously manipulated by cruel predators.

The portly man arrived at the driver's side door and leaned down to take a peek inside Pete's car, playing the beam of a flashlight over the interior. He had greasy, unruly hair and a jowly, rosy-cheeked face. He wore a black long-sleeved shirt and a pair of baggy black jeans. A device that looked like it was probably a stun gun was clipped to his belt, as was a pair of handcuffs. There was no sign of a gun, which seemed strange.

The man's flat expression was devoid of emotion of any kind. He looked first at Pete and then at the woman slumped down in his passenger seat, his gaze lingering there a moment before returning to Pete. "Something wrong with your lady friend?"

Pete nervously cleared his throat. "Um ..."

He didn't know whether to come clean right away or delay the inevitable moment of discovery as long as possible. Delay seemed pointless under the circumstances, but he couldn't bring himself to just blurt out, "She's dead."

The man's flat expression sharpened a small degree, taking on an aspect that might have indicated genuine concern for the woman's well-being or merely a mild curiosity. It was hard to tell with this guy. "Is she … drunk?"

Pete forced out a nervous laugh. "Um … yeah. She's, uh, totally blasted out of her mind. Had a wild night on the town, I guess you could say. That's why she's almost naked." Pete started to feel inspired and decided to elaborate a bit further. "Yeah, man, she did something like thirteen shots of tequila and decided to strip down to her undies right there in the middle of the bar."

The man scratched his chin. "Hmm. What's your relationship to the lady? Friend? Boyfriend? Something else?"

"Um … friend?"

Pete hated the way the word came out, with that emphasis at the end that made it sound like a question. A declaration like that needed to be made with certainty when dealing with a cop.

A corner of the man's mouth twitched, a hint of a smirk. "You don't sound so sure."

Pete coughed. "Oh, I'm sure. I'm sorry. I'm just always nervous around cops, even for minor traffic stops. I'm definitely her friend and not her boyfriend."

The man grunted. "I should think not. She's out of your league for sure."

Pete laughed. "I agree. Absolutely."

The man craned his head around for a better look at the dead woman. After a moment of silent appraisal, his brow creased in a frown. His eyes flicked toward Pete. "Lower the window on that side, please."

Pete bit back a whimper. "But—"

The man stepped back and aimed his flashlight right at Pete's face, making him squint. "Right now. Or I'm putting you in cuffs and placing you under arrest while I investigate further."

Shit.

For a few wondrous moments there, Pete had allowed himself to believe he might be able to finesse his way out of this situation, but now the jig was clearly up. Saying nothing else, he thumbed the button that lowered the passenger side window.

The portly man glared at him. "Stay where you are. Any funny business and you'll be in a world of hurt, my friend. A world of hurt."

Pete nodded to show his understanding, but again said nothing. What was there to say? The portly cop was moments away from learning the grim truth of the situation, at which point things would get loads more tense and dramatic. And there was nothing he could do about it other than sit back and wait for it to happen.

He frowned as he watched the man waddle around the front of his car. Now that the guy was no longer right in his face, it hit him how off certain things about him seemed. He didn't look like any cop Pete had ever seen, plainclothes or otherwise. The man was morbidly obese, but the sense of something wrong was more than just about his weight. It was everything about him. His unkempt appearance. The strange flatness of his demeanor. His clothes didn't look like the kind any cop would wear, not even a detective. They looked like the clothes a person intent on skulking around and doing shady things in the night would wear. And even Pete knew the man wasn't following anything remotely recognizable as standard police protocol. He hadn't said anything about why he'd pulled Pete over, nor had he asked him to produce any identification.

Now Pete was thinking about the loud creak the door to the man's car had made when he got out of it. He doubted a police vehicle of any recent vintage would make a sound like that. No, that was the sound the door of a junked-up old beater would make. That got him to thinking about the rest of it. The dome light. The lack of a sidearm.

Fuck!

Pete sat up straight behind the wheel as the answer to the mystery came to him.

He's a fake fucking cop. Holy shit!

Pete had heard stories about guys like this before. Cop groupies or wannabes who got their kicks by buying some of the gear and prowling around, pretending to be the real thing, sometimes even pulling people over and harassing them. That was exactly what this was. He didn't even need the guy to confirm it for him. He felt it in his gut.

The fake cop had arrived at the passenger side window. He reached in and gave the dead woman's shoulder a little nudge. When she didn't react, he glanced at Pete, smirking. "Dead to the world, ain't she?"

He chuckled.

Pete swallowed hard and said nothing.

The man shifted the flashlight beam away from the woman's face, angling it now to illuminate her enormous breasts. His mouth dropped open and he licked his lips. "Nice jugs."

He reached in and cupped one of her breasts with a pudgy hand, squeezing and kneading it a moment before sliding some of his stubby, sausage-like fingers beneath the cup of her bra. Pete clenched his teeth and trembled with fury, wondering how long he should let this go on before intervening. If he'd had any lingering doubts regarding the man's lack of official law enforcement status, they were now thoroughly erased.

Then the man paused in his molestation of the woman he apparently still believed was just a passed-out drunk. Something subtle had changed in the set of his features. Pete sensed he wasn't yet truly alarmed but had suddenly intuited that something wasn't quite right.

He took his hand away from her breast and pitched his voice louder than before, as if he could rouse her through sheer volume. "Miss, are you okay? Have you been drinking tonight, ma'am?" He leaned a little closer, sniffing the air in his piggy way. "Strange, I don't smell any booze on her breath. In fact …" He held a hand in front of her mouth, his frown deepening after a moment. He put his hand to her throat to check for a pulse. "Shit. She's dead."

He looked at Pete and they held each other's gaze for a moment that seemed to stretch out forever, a spell that didn't break until Pete reached for the door handle on his side. The man took off running in the direction of his car. Pete got out and chased after him, primitive instinct driving him as he dragged the folding knife out of his pocket. He was an animal, acting only to survive, with no conscious thought of what he was doing. If he *had* stopped to think about it, the fake cop might have gotten the upper hand. For once in his life, his slight build gave him an advantage over an adversary. He moved much faster than the other man, who stumbled as he neared his car and fell heavily across the hood. Pete saw him fumbling with the stun gun. He was trying desperately to unclip it from his belt, but his trembling fingers betrayed him. He couldn't grip it right. Pete swatted his hand away and opened the knife.

"Please," the man said. "Please. I won't tell nobody. I swear."

Pete said, "I'm sorry. I never wanted it to come to this."

Then he rammed the big blade into the man's temple up to the hilt.

TWENTY-ONE

The storage facility looked deserted as Pete pulled into the parking lot. He saw what looked like the main office, a small building accessible to anyone paying a visit. The rest of the facility with its multiple rows of individual storage units was encircled by a tall fence with thick metal bars. No lights were on inside the office building, but a black SUV with tinted windows was parked at the door. As best Pete could tell, there were no other vehicles on the premises. Aside from his own car, of course.

He took out his phone and sent Mary a text: I'M HERE.

Seconds later, he saw her name appear on the screen. He put the phone to his ear just in time to hear her say, "You are two minutes late."

Pete grunted. "I was delayed again. But, hey, I'm here, with the package in tow as directed. That's all that really matters, right?"

"I suppose."

His text chime sounded.

Pete took the phone away from his ear and looked at the screen. The message was from Mary and consisted only of a four-digit number.

He put the phone to his ear again. "What's with the numbers?"

"That's the gate code, genius. Ride up to the gate and enter it in the keypad. Like magic, the gate will open. Proceed to unit 167. We'll see you soon."

She ended the call.

Pete put the phone away and drove up to the gate. He entered the code she'd provided and, as promised, the gate slid open. After steering his car through the opening, he pulled to a stop and listened to the rattle of the gate sliding back into place. There were units to either side of him. A spotlight was mounted above each of the orange rollup doors. The unit to his right was number 010. He took his foot off the brake and tapped the gas pedal, allowing his car to roll slowly forward. His head was on a swivel the whole time he spent navigating the maze of storage units, his eyes searching for signs of anyone lurking in the shadows. The complex was larger than the first impression he'd formed of it driving up to it in the dark. The dark was deceptive. It hid things. Obscured them. The nighttime was a friend to thieves, murderers, and everyone else up to no good.

I'm one of those people now, Pete thought. *A villain. A murderer. A bad person.*

Until his fateful encounter with the fake cop, a big part of the way Pete had dealt with the madness of it all was by clinging to the belief that he was essentially innocent. That he was a victim and nothing more. Well, that had changed. He had taken a life. There was no taking it back. Sure, it could be argued he'd acted in self-defense, in the name of basic survival, but that was stretching the truth of the matter quite a bit and he knew it. No matter what else happened from here, he was changed irrevocably. His soul was tainted. The knowledge made him want to scream and cry and rage against the world. Instead, he did none of those things. He remained numb within his new cocoon of detachment as he took turn after turn and finally arrived at unit 167.

A car that looked empty at first glance was parked off to the side, alongside the door to the opposite unit. This gave Pete enough room to pull up and park in front of the designated unit. The other car was a four-door Lexus sedan. He'd never seen the steel-gray vehicle before, but had a hunch it was the same car he'd caught glimpses of during the Facetime conversations with Mary. Unit 167's rollup door had been raised and a light was on inside. The light was from a powerful electric lantern, bright enough to make Pete squint against the harsh glare of its bulb. The lantern had been placed atop a black card table. An open laptop computer sat near the lantern on the table's surface. A single metal folding chair was positioned on the floor near the table.

Mary, now wearing a black trench coat and a black hat with a broad brim tilted partly over her face, was sitting in the chair with her legs crossed. She got to her feet as Pete got out of his car and came around to the passenger side. The gun she'd threatened him with before was in her hand again, its barrel aimed at his midsection.

She waved him aside with a flick of her hand. "Move over. Let me see her."

Pete sidestepped out of the way, allowing Mary an unobstructed look at the body slumped in his passenger seat. She stared at the corpse a silent moment and then flicked her gun hand at him again. "Get her out of there. Bring her in here."

Before he could begin to comply with this directive, Pete was distracted by something at the back of the storage unit. Something that, until now, had been obscured by his focus on Mary and the bright light from the lantern. He'd detected an unpleasant odor upon getting out of his car, but had not immediately been able to identify what it was. Now he understood. The bodies of two more dead women clad only in sexy underwear and platform heels had been dumped haphazardly there in the back. The unpleasant odor was the onset of rot.

Pete gave Mary a deeply perplexed look. "Okay, I'm sorry, but I have to ask. What in the holy blue fucking hell do you have against strippers? Did a band of machine-gun-toting stripper terrorists massacre your whole family when you were a child? Or is it some kind of radical statement about the objectification of women in modern society? If it's the latter, I'd say there are probably more effective ways of getting your point across. Seriously, what gives?"

Mary gave him a long look of simmering anger before tersely replying, "Not that it is any of your business, but childhood trauma is indeed at the root of it, as is the hatred I've always harbored for my whore mother. Infer from that whatever you wish. Back to the matter at hand. I told you—"

She was interrupted by the sound of a car door opening. Pete turned around and saw Shane Watson emerge from the back of the Lexus. Pete could swear the car had been empty as he'd pulled up outside the unit, but he supposed Shane had stayed out of sight by stretching out across the backseat. The other man grinned when he saw Pete. "There he is! The Wildman. Hey, man, you ever think of getting into the stunt-driving business? I only ask because you're a natural at that shit. With your skills, you could get work in one of those *Fast and Furious* movies. Anyway, just a suggestion. Think about it, bro."

Shane's face had been scrubbed clean and, like Mary, he'd changed out of the clothes he'd been wearing earlier, switching them out for a black track suit and black sneakers. His blond hair was mostly hidden beneath a black baseball cap, the front of which was unadorned with any kind of logo.

Pete cocked an eyebrow, eyeing him in a curious way. "You're in a chipper mood."

Shane shrugged as he moved past Pete and stepped into the storage unit, taking up a position alongside Mary. "What can I say, man? It's been an amazing night. Maybe the most amazing night of my life. And I owe it all to this little lady right here." Still grinning, he draped an arm over her shoulders and gave her a squeeze, making Mary wince in obvious discomfort. "Isn't she something?"

Pete's quizzical look gave way to a frown. "Huh. There seems to have been a radical shift in your attitude about ... well, *everything* since the last time I saw you."

Shane nodded, laughing. "Yeah, uh, about that ... look, I'm sorry, man, but a lot of that shit was pure put-on. It was just more bullshit to mess with your head. I've been working with Mary on this project of hers from the beginning. I did all that batshit crazy stuff because I *wanted* to, not because she was forcing me to do it." He leaned forward slightly, cupping a hand around his mouth to speak in a mock-conspiratorial way. "And let me tell you something, just between us guys, you ever get another chance to pork a dead chick, take it. That shit was the bomb. Huge fucking rush. And, bonus, they never get mouthy."

He howled laughter.

Pete's face twisted in disgust. "I think I'll pass."

Shane snorted. "Don't get all judgmental on me, man." He smirked. "Besides, it's not like you're ever actually gonna have another shot at it. Or at anything else."

A chill went through Pete at those last words.

Mary abruptly shrugged out of Shane's overbearing embrace and pushed him away. "Enough fucking around. We're on a schedule here." She waved the gun at Pete again. "Bring the dead slut in here."

"Are you going to kill me?"

She raised the gun, aiming it at his face. "I'll shoot you where you stand if you don't do what I told you to fucking do right fucking now."

Despite the dire nature of this threat, Pete did not immediately obey. He believed she would kill him if he didn't do what she wanted. What made him hesitate was the abrupt change in her voice. Prior to just now, he'd always heard her speak in the same bland, vaguely mid-American accent, but there'd been no trace of that in this latest utterance. Pete wasn't the most worldly man ever. He hadn't traveled a lot. He had, however, watched a lot of Hollywood espionage movies set in faraway locations. She sounded like a sexy foreign agent in one of those movies, someone who could be from eastern Europe. Was Russia a part of eastern Europe? He thought it probably was.

Judging from Shane's astonished expression, he was just as taken aback by the change. "What ... the ... fuck?"

Mary glanced back and forth between them in obvious exasperation for a moment. Then she appeared to belatedly realize what had happened. Before she even said another word, Pete understood that what they'd just heard was her real accent. He also understood that everything about Mary was a sham. A lie. And in a moment of extreme exasperation, she'd finally broken character.

She shook her head in apparent self-disgust. "Fuck it."

She spun toward Shane, aimed the gun, and fired twice. One

bullet punched through his forehead while the second put a hole straight through the center of his face. A spray of blood and brains emerged from the bigger exit wounds at the back of his head. Shane staggered backward and fell against the wall, collapsing to the concrete floor an instant later.

The gun immediately swung back toward Pete. "You have one last chance to do what I have already fucking told you to do."

The fake American accent was back in place. Strangely, its return now felt even more jarring than the original slipup. Pete had so many questions, but he chose to keep them to himself. The woman had just killed the man who claimed to be her equal partner in this thing. She surely wouldn't hesitate to kill him if he caused her any additional aggravation.

He nodded and turned away from her.

He went to his car and opened the door on the passenger side. Reaching in, he took hold of the dead woman under her arms and dragged her out of the car and into the storage unit. At Mary's direction, he dragged her all the way to the back of the unit, depositing the corpse in a corner.

She pointed the gun at the card table. "Sit there."

Pete sighed and did as instructed, sliding the folding chair over to the table and taking a seat in front of the open laptop computer, which he saw now was his own computer. In the midst of all the craziness of the night, he somehow hadn't realized it had gone missing. A glance at the lower right corner of the screen told him it was connected to a wi-fi network in the vicinity. The browser was displaying a page from his bank's website. His savings account, specifically.

Mary placed the muzzle of the gun against the back of his head. "You have $41,569.83 in your savings account, the bulk of it deriving from a modest inheritance you received after the death of one of your uncles."

Pete cleared his throat. "How do you know so much about me? I never told you that."

Mary grunted. "I make it my business to learn such things." She pressed the muzzle harder against the back of his head. "I have already set up a transfer from your account to one of my own. When the transfer is complete, I will reroute the funds to another account, and then to another. They will disappear without a trace. I want you to press the transfer button to initiate the transaction."

Pete frowned. "What?"

She grunted. "You heard me, stupid boy. I'm taking all of your money. It's not a fortune, but it should fund the beginning of my next adventure quite nicely."

Pete twisted his head around to look at her. "Oh, I get that you're ripping me off. You obviously have world-class hacking skills. Among many other skills, I'm sure. You could have done this yourself already and been on your way to wherever you're going next ages ago. Why make me do it?"

She smiled. "Why do you think? To complete your humiliation, of course. To make you give me your money. Because it's *fun.*"

Pete shook his head. "You're crazy."

Mary rapped the butt of the gun against the side of his head. "Do it now. I've told you all I'll ever tell you about why I did any of this." She grabbed him by the hair at the back of his head and forced him to face the laptop's screen again. "Press the fucking button."

Pete's forefinger hovered over the laptop's touchpad. He couldn't stop shaking because he had no doubt Mary—or whatever her real name was—was seconds away from murdering him. His other hand was under the table, reaching for the stun gun he'd taken off the fake cop after killing him. It was tucked inside the waistband of his jeans and hidden by the bottom of his loose T-shirt. He had no confidence in his ability to get to it and effectively wield it before having his brainpan emptied by Mary, but he had to try. He had no other choice. At least the gun was no longer pressed to the back of his head. It might give him an extra precious second or two to get the stun gun out and turn around before she could shoot him. The hand beneath the table was just a few inches away from the stun gun when he felt a stinging sensation in his neck.

Slapping his neck and crying out in pain, Pete twisted around and saw the hypodermic needle held loosely between the fingers of Mary's right hand. The gun had been put away.

Sliding numbly out of the chair, he landed on his back on the cold floor. His vision was blurry and his thoughts were rapidly turning muddy. He looked up and saw Mary looming over him.

He managed to rasp out a single shuddery inquiry: "Was …

poison?"

Mary smiled inscrutably and said nothing.

Pete groaned.

Everything went black.

When consciousness began to return some time later, his head felt thick and his thoughts were sluggish. His vision was too blurry to make out much initially, except that the lantern was still on in the storage unit. A great blob of light obscured everything else in those first moments back.

He soon became aware of other things, though, all of them disturbing in the extreme. There was a weight atop him, pinning him to the floor. It felt like some other person was lying on top of him. He tried shifting out from beneath the other person, but found he was unable to move. As his vision came into sharper focus, he realized the weight pinning him to the floor was dead woman number two. Her remaining undergarments had been removed. All his clothes had been removed. But that wasn't the worst of it.

The worst part was that someone—Mary, he assumed—had used a tremendous amount of duct tape to bind them limb to limb. He was completely immobilized. Pete tried to scream, but couldn't due to the obstruction in his mouth. He twisted his head around and saw Shane's bloody corpse propped against a wall. At some point while Pete had been unconscious, Mary had stripped Shane's corpse of its clothing. Where his genitals should have been was nothing but a gaping, bloody ruin of shredded flesh.

Pete tried screaming again, and again was foiled in the attempt. It took hours of trying to finally expel the obstruction from his throat.

By then he was almost too tired to scream.

EPILOGUE

The elegantly dressed woman in seat 32B on United Flight 919 was traveling under an assumed name, a name that matched the name on the passport she was currently using. That name was not Mary Wilson, the name she'd used for the last year and a half while orchestrating her latest project. The alias was also not Irina Leskova, which was her birth name. No one had called her Irina for close to ten years. As far as anyone who had known her in that long ago life knew, Irina was dead.

This did not make her sad. She had been reborn so many times and was set to begin yet another new life shortly, this time in London as Sophia Wentworth. She didn't know everything about Sophia yet. Her new creation was a work in progress. Crafting these new identities was half the fun of it. Before she identified her next victim, however, Sophia would be a perfect, seamless work of art. There would be nothing to tip off authorities or anyone else to the truth about her. For now, the primary differences were aesthetic. Mary Wilson's retro-chic blonde hair was gone. In its place, a jet-black mane in a more stylishly modern cut. The professional attire of an office drone had been replaced by a more fashion-savvy sensibility. The rest of it—Sophia's personality and background—would come in time.

She did the things she did because the life she'd lived as Irina had bored her, though most would have found her profession an exciting one. Even a relatively exotic profession is still a profession, bound by rules and performance expectations. The woman wanted to live life only on her own terms. And she wanted to play with people and hurt them in fundamental, profound ways, a thing that could only be achieved by fully integrating herself into their lives for a time. With the professional skills gleaned from her years of training, she was able to do this easily. By design, her targets were always small and insignificant people. She stayed away from wealthy and high-profile individuals so as not to provoke interest from the wrong agencies.

The hum of the plane's engines grew louder as the aircraft began to pull away from the terminal. It wasn't quite time for takeoff, though. The woman still had time to glance through the tabloid newspaper she'd purchased from a kiosk in the airport. She loved the sensational tabloids above all other news publications, with the way they focused on the most lurid stories. The cover headlines were often hilarious. Today's headline for this particular tabloid was a prime example—DEAD STRIPPER

STORAGE.

The huge font filled the page.

The woman once known as Irina wasn't sure why she'd left Pete Adler alive. She was a pure sociopath with no discernible conscience and thus never felt any remorse for the many lives she'd ended over the years. But there had been something about Pete that made him even more pathetic than her usual targets, a quality that made her think it would be better to spare his life and let him live with the memory of the many humiliating and horrible things that had happened to him. She sensed this would be worse for him than it would be for the average person.

Far worse.

Just thinking about it made her smile.

A chime sounded and the plane's captain spoke over the intercom. They were now taxiing out to the runway. Passengers were instructed to buckle their seatbelts and return table trays to the full upright and locked position. The woman tucked the tabloid in the seat pouch in front of her. Her seatbelt was already fastened. She felt the usual rush of excitement that was always there at the beginning of each of these rebirths. It was as close as she ever came to experiencing real joy.

In another ten minutes, the plane was in the air. Deeper into its journey, as it flew high above international waters, the woman in seat 32B fell into a doze and dreamed contentedly of violent and bloody things, visions of the recent past and glorious portents of things to come.

ACKNOWLEDGMENTS

First off, I have to acknowledge the obvious influence of Quentin Tarantino. The title of this book derives from a phrase uttered by one of the minor characters in his classic film *Pulp Fiction*, substituting the word "stripper" for the original, far more offensive slur. I'd also like to thank C.V. Hunt and Andersen Prunty for bringing me into the Grindhouse Press fold. My writing has occasionally been described as "grindhouse-like". So this makes it official. I'm definitely a Grindhouse writer now. Thanks also to my awesome wife, Jenn, who continues to make life far more fun and interesting than it would otherwise be. Then there's the usual suspects. Brian Keene, Mike Lombardo, Tod Clark, Paul Legerski, Ryan Harding, Matt Hayward, etc. And the dozens of others whose names I don't feel like typing out because this thing is already too long. You know who you are. Let's all get together for beers and a Big Kahuna burger sometime soon.

ABOUT THE AUTHOR

Bryan Smith is the author of numerous novels and novellas, including *68 Kill*, *Slowly We Rot*, *Depraved*, *The Killing Kind*, *The Freakshow*, and *Last Day*. Bestselling horror author Brian Keene described *Slowly We Rot* as, "The best zombie novel I've ever read." A film version of *68 Kill*, directed by Trent Haaga and starring Matthew Gray Gubler from *Criminal Minds*, was released in 2017. Bryan lives in Tennessee with his wife, Jennifer, and their many pets.

Follow him on Twitter at @Bryan_D_Smith and on Facebook at https://www.facebook.com/bryansmith/

Other Grindhouse Press Titles

#666__*Satanic Summer* by Andersen Prunty

#040__*Triple Axe* by Scott Cole

#039__*Scummer* by John Wayne Comunale

#038__*Cockblock* by C.V. Hunt

#037__*Irrationalia* by Andersen Prunty

#036__*Full Brutal* by Kristopher Triana

#035__*Office Mutant* by Pete Risley

#034__*Death Pacts and Left-Hand Paths* by John Wayne Comunale

#033__*Home Is Where the Horror Is* by C.V. Hunt

#032__*This Town Needs A Monster* by Andersen Prunty

#031__*The Fetishists* by A.S. Coomer

#030__*Ritualistic Human Sacrifice* by C.V. Hunt

#029__*The Atrocity Vendor* by Nick Cato

#028__*Burn Down the House and Everyone In It* by Zachary T. Owen

#027__*Misery and Death and Everything Depressing* by C.V. Hunt

#026__*Naked Friends* by Justin Grimbol

#025__*Ghost Chant* by Gina Ranalli

#024__*Hearers of the Constant Hum* by William Pauley III

#023__*Hell's Waiting Room* by C.V. Hunt

#022__*Creep House: Horror Stories* by Andersen Prunty

#021__*Other People's Shit* by C.V. Hunt

#020__*The Party Lords* by Justin Grimbol

#019__*Sociopaths In Love* by Andersen Prunty

#018__*The Last Porno Theater* by Nick Cato

#017__*Zombieville* by C.V. Hunt

#016__*Samurai Vs. Robo-Dick* by Steve Lowe

www.ingramcontent.com/pod-product-compliance
Lightning Source LLC
Chambersburg PA
CBHW011456170626
46814CB00009B/3071

* 9 7 8 1 9 4 1 9 1 8 3 3 3 *